Tombstones

BEEKMAN HILLS

KC ENDERS

ISBN-13: 979-8432030573

Tombstones

BEEKMAN HILLS

To family.
By blood or by other means, you are my reason.

1

Kate

How many frogs does *a person have to kiss before she finds her—*

Who am I kidding? I'm not even looking for a prince at this point, just someone who's a little less toad than what I've found on Tinder, Bumble, and all the other dating sites.

I sit across the café table from tonight's frog, sipping my wine, and I look, really look, at this guy. He's taller than me, just barely. Works out, probably too much because that really is a thing. Dude is stacked with gym muscle, finely honed and aesthetically pleasing in the body-builder-Instagram-profile sort of way. He's dressed nice, he doesn't smell bad, and he hasn't picked his nose or anything, but may the good Lord help me, I might just die of boredom right here in this chair. I don't have even the slightest clue what he's droning on about. I tried, really tried, to follow the conversation, but when my mind starts wandering and the first thing that pops into my head is whether or not I cleaned the turtle cage in my classroom, I feel like that's a sign from up above to cut my losses and move on.

What might I have to do to make this dude stop talking and pay the bill, so I can just go home? Let's be real; there's a part of me that's wondering if he's going to cough up the cash for the bill or if I'll be the one paying. That nonsense has happened to me far too many times in the past year.

"Excuse me. I'm just going to run to the girls' room real quick," I say, sliding my chair back from the table.

All I get in return is a quick nod, more of a chin lift if I'm being honest, and the frog date goes back to his phone. If he's smart, he'll be trolling Tinder while I'm gone to set up a sure thing for later because the only thing I'm sure of is that this is a one-and-done. That the role of tonight's good-night kiss will be played by the shaking of hands and moving the fuck on.

The tiny restroom is full of other Friday night dates, and while I wait my turn, I create each of their fictional backstories to entertain myself. The chick at the sink grabs my attention, and with her huge purse/overnight bag splayed open, she's either getting paid to be on her date or hoping she reaps some similar payoff. Or maybe she's a Boy Scout wannabe, perpetually prepared for any emergency. She could probably save a small Third World country with what she's packing in that bag.

A stall opens up, and I do my business as quickly as I can. Not that I'm in any hurry to get back out to the Frog

Prince, but I feel for the very pregnant mama-to-be who's wedged herself into the cramped room. If there weren't three angry-looking girls between me and her, I'd have let her skip to the front of the line. But New York girls are way different from what one might find in Hattiesburg, Mississippi. Maybe I should go back home. Lord knows that state could do with some more teachers.

I love my students here in New York though. The past couple of years, I've gotten to know so many families, and I want the chance to teach the younger siblings of my kiddos. Or at least watch them come on through kindergarten.

I thoroughly wash my hands. Twice, just to kill some extra time because, let's be honest, I really don't want to go back out there. I contemplate waiting until the pregnant lady comes out, so I can congratulate her, ask about the baby, pretend for just a moment that I'm next. But that would be creepy and weird. I might have a touch of baby fever but not enough to have a restraining order slapped on me for randomly stalking pregnant baby mamas in public restrooms.

With a fresh coat of red on my lips and a cursory fluff of the blonde beach waves I labored over for this stupid date, I go back to the dining room, only to find the Frog Prince exchanging phones with the chick from the restroom, the one with the huge bag and desperation spilling off of her.

"Took care of the check while you were gone. You ready to get out of here?" he asks, throwing his napkin on the table. He hikes his pants high on his hips, almost past his navel, and moves toward the front of the restaurant. "You, uh ... you need me to call you a cab or ..."

"I'm good, thanks." I pluck a valet ticket from my bag and hand it off the moment I'm out the door. I pull a couple of dollars from my wallet and press it into the valet's hand, letting him know I'm in a hurry. Actually, I'm desperate to get out of here. Turning to the frog, I paste a polite smile on my face the way my mama taught me. "Thank you for dinner. It was lovely meeting you." I leave the statement dangling in the air between us, hoping, praying that this night will end here. Now. Done.

"Okay, so I'm going to bolt, Kasey. It was great, really. I, uh ..." He shifts his weight, gunning for his escape. "So, you want me to call you or ..."

I don't bother to correct him on my name; there's no need. "Not necessary. You take care now," I say, reining in the bless your heart that is begging for release.

Thankfully, the valet pulls up and holds open my car door. I slide behind the wheel and let out a sigh of relief, one much like I imagine a deer lets go of when a bullet whizzes past, missing him by a mile. And then the gun jams. And the hunter falls out of the tree. That kind of relief.

Something has got to give. I can't keep dating these assholes. There has got to be some real men left out there for a girl. I don't need a prince or a knight in shining armor. Just a regular person, one with manners. And, if he happens to fill out a pair of jeans just right, that'd be fine, too.

Streetlights blink through the car's interior as I drive

toward my apartment. I have no desire to go home. None. My roommate, Gracyn, is gone, down in the city for her first client visit since starting with her dad's accounting firm. Our apartment is far too quiet when she's not there.

Quiet and lonely. And I just can't, not yet. I take a left at the next intersection, and three blocks down, I turn into the parking lot of McBride's Public House. Park. Purse. Phone. Patrón? Maybe that should be the drink of my night.

Pushing through the door, I sidle up to the bar and claim the one empty seat at the corner. "Finn, we're drowning my sorrows," I say, dropping into the barstool. "I'm gonna need a shot of the good stuff with a chaser of his friends."

"Grand. You're ready for the whiskey then?" The redheaded bartender's brogue carries over the din of conversation filling the air. He snaps a coaster down in front of me and grabs a couple of shot glasses. Lining them up in a pretty little row, like soldiers marching off to war, Finn O'Meara places both hands on the bar and dares me to make a change. Dares me with a wink and a smile, knowing full well that it's not going to happen.

"Sweet boy, no. I need Señor Patrón, my friend. He's the only one for me, the only man who hasn't let me down yet."

Finn nods, reaching high on the shelf behind the bar, past the rows of Irish whiskey and brandy. Past the high-end vodka and gin. Sitting pretty in the middle of the back row, closest to the lights, is the squat bottle with the lime-green ribbon lovingly wrapped around its neck. That's the one for me. In fact, I'm pretty sure that I'm the only one who drinks it.

"So, you had another date then?" Finn asks as he pours the fiery liquid into the glasses. He pauses, waiting to see just how bad my date tonight was.

I nod at the third shot glass, giving him the go-ahead. "I did, and it was at least three tequilas bad." A hint of honey tickles my senses as I lift the glass, savoring that moment in time where it's all sweet promises and anticipation. Tipping back the first glass erases all illusions of grandeur. Reality sets in as the peppery blast burns its way down the back of my throat. Cleansing me.

By the time shot number three slides past my lips, the demons of my most recent dating disaster have just about been exorcised.

2

___

Jack

J UST THIRTY DAYS STATESIDE, and then we'll be back in the sandbox for another six months. Not enough time to do all the things I want to do at home. Not enough time to see all the people I need to see, but I've got to plant my feet on American soil again. That simple act will somehow ground me enough to make it through my final tour in the desert. Not having to shake sand out of fucking everything for that time alone is worth the price of the plane ticket.

Steak. First thing I want to do is get a big-ass steak, medium rare. Wash it down with an ice-cold IPA and maybe, if the mood strikes, a fresh bright green Caesar salad. Croutons, sharp Parmesan, and creamy, tangy dressing. Forget a reprieve from the sand. Food is worth the damn plane ticket.

"I'll drop you at your house and take off for a bit. Give

you and the fam some time together. Get reacquainted," I tell my best friend, Dallas "Tripp" Triplett. My brother in arms. I steer the rental car onto the parkway and head north toward Beekman Hills.

"Like hell you will," he drawls, adjusting the satellite radio to an alternative rock station. "Chloe'll kill me if I let you leave. And don't even with Jake, man. That boy'll tear you up if he has to wait any longer to see you."

I'm not worried about Chloe. I know she loves me, but she's not about to harm a hair on her husband's head once she gets her hands on him again. But their son, Jake? Totally different story.

That kid has a serious case of hero worship that doesn't make a lick of sense. His dad is just as badass as me, if not more so. But, for some crazy-ass reason, Jake looks up to me; he is completely obsessed with me.

"You want me to take Jake out for a burger or something? Give you and Chloe time to—"

"Nah, man," Tripp cuts me off. "Come in. Have a beer and get settled. You know she's made a ton of food for us, and it'd break her heart if you bolted. Really."

I check my blind spot and press the gas pedal down, passing a string of slow-moving vehicles. They're probably doing the speed limit, but I don't have time for that shit. I have a lot to pack into a short stint—a lot that I need privacy for—and I'm not wasting a precious second puttering along on a perfectly good highway. Hell, my team moves faster than this over shitty sandy roads while searching for IEDs.

"Fine. I'll come in, have dinner, and say hello, but I'm

not staying with you. You need time with your family, man, and I need time alone. All by my lonesome." I glance over at Tripp, dead serious and not willing to give an inch. "I don't even want to consider the possibility of hearing your sorry ass snoring for the next month, so don't fight me on it. Not negotiable."

"Fine," he says, the matter done.

TRIPP SNAPS AWAKE AS I bump the car into his driveway, gravel crunching loudly under the tires.

"Damn. Fell asleep," he grunts, as if I hadn't noticed.

The windows of the car have been rattling for the past half hour. It never ceases to amaze me how he can lock that shit down when we're in the field, but the minute he knows everything is squared away, he lets loose. I haven't slept like that in longer than I can remember—probably the eight damn years since my plebe year at West Point when I went home for Christmas break. That was the sleep of the dead. No stolen naps, no bracing for the upper classes, no pinging or squaring corners. Just quiet, blissful sleep when my pop wasn't dragging my ass out to run fence line.

The front door flies open as the car rolls to a stop spilling Jake out into the yard, followed by Tripp's hunting dog, Bronson. Tripp throws open the door and scoops his boy up into his arms as the white-and-black-dappled hound dog bounces around him, demanding his own slice of attention.

"You're home, Dad. You're really home," Jake screeches.

He's so overcome; the poor kid is on the verge of tears. And the dog? Bronson is beside himself, hopping around and squealing almost as much as Jake.

After a tight hug, during which my friend somehow completes the transformation from Special Forces sergeant to dad and husband, Tripp says, "And guess who I brought with me."

Jake leans back from his dad and narrows his big brown eyes at the car, searching. Darkness of the fall evening keeps me mostly hidden in shadow, and before long, Jake is squirming to get out of his father's grasp.

Just as his little feet hit solid ground, I open the driver's door and step out of the car, beaming at the kid.

"Uncle Jack."

The volume he's capable of producing is unreal, but I know from experience that I've got to be on the ball now or else my balls are getting nailed. And not in a good way.

Jake launches himself at me, running full throttle, no brakes in sight. I pivot just a hair and brace for impact. Sure, I could pick him up before he gets to me, but this run-and-hug thing has become part of our shtick. It's just that Jake has grown, and a man, home on leave, has to protect his goods from the wrong kind of overzealous greetings. Specifically, the exuberant greetings of children of unfortunate height. Yeah, I've been head-butted in the junk before, and that shit is for sure something I don't ever want to experience again.

"Hey, little dude," I say, letting him hug me for all he's worth.

This kid holds my heart in his sweaty little hands, and I couldn't begin to tell you the *why*s or *how*s of it. It just is.

The vise grip around my body loosens enough for me to crouch down to eye-level with my namesake. Well, my sort-of namesake. As much of an honor as it was for them to want to name their kid after me, the Wyatt Jacksons from my father on back were nothing but overbearing assholes. Hell, I don't like sharing a name with the old bastards, so Tripp and Chloe flipped what my parents gave me, hopefully breaking the cycle of asshole, and Jacob Wyatt Triplett has been my man ever since.

"Tell me something good, Jake," I prompt.

His eyes go wide with all the seriousness a five-year-old can muster. "You're home. And my dad is home. And you can be my lunch buddy at school every day." His excitement starts to build again, and the motor on his mouth is about to kick into high gear. "And you can meet my friends. I tell them about you all the time. And my teacher, Miss Beard, she's the best and you can see my seat and my cubby and ... and ..."

"Jake, baby, let's let Uncle Jack and Daddy in the house, you think?" Chloe calls from the front steps, Tripp's arms wrapped casually around her.

They do the whole separation-reunion thing with style and grace. Never making those around them feel as though they're in the way or that they are desperate for a private reunion. They just fall back into absolute normalcy.

"Hey, Chloe," I greet, straightening up and ruffling Jake's sandy hair. "You look gorgeous, as always." I climb the steps and pull her into a hug. "When are you gonna get smart and leave this bas—sorry—bad boy for a real man?"

"You couldn't handle me, Jack"—she swats my chest—"and I wouldn't know what to do without Tripp. Now, grab your kit bags and come in, so I can feed you."

The look Tripp gives me screams, *You tell her*, as he hustles down to the car and pops the trunk, grabbing both of our bags. And then he kicks the lid onto my coffin. "Where do you want me to put this, Jack? In the house or in your truck?"

"The house," Chloe says as I call, "Truck."

Chloe props her hands on her hips and hits me with the mom look, her bright blue eyes narrowing.

"Truck," I say again with more determination. "Chloe, you know I love you—all of you—but you need family time, and I need some solitude."

"But, Jack—"

"I appreciate the offer—you know I do—but a man has needs."

She shakes her head, laughing softly as Tripp joins us again.

"And I need some relief from this man's ridiculous snoring. This is the official transfer of custody. I don't want him back for a month."

Chloe ushers us all into the house, the scent of home cooking in the air. "Jack, you know you're family, and you're welcome in our home. You can't stay in a hotel for the entire month. What are you going to do there, all alone?"

"Actually, I can, and you don't wanna know, darlin'." I

chuckle. "Now, tell me what smells so good before I die a starving man."

Jake runs ahead, into the kitchen, and pulls out his chair, plopping down onto the seat. "Mom made roast and potatoes and gravy. And chocolate cake and ice cream, if you eat all your dinner. Uncle Jack, you get to sit by me, so Mommy and Daddy can hold hands while they eat." His little face wrinkles up in disgust at the idea.

Tripp pulls a couple of beers from the fridge, handing me one and drinking deep from the other. We tuck into the meal that Chloe made, warming us from the inside out, filling our stomachs, and welcoming us home. Conversation is light and decidedly normal during dinner with Jake telling us all about going to school, his friends, and the best teacher in the world, and Chloe sharing her thoughts on a group of moms she refers to as Teacup Terrorists, trying to run playdates with an iron fist.

The evening drifts easily, and with full bellies, we all get a little sleepy. Well, Jake and I do. He's on my lap, head tucked into my chest, eyes getting heavy.

"Chloe, you want me to put him to bed?" I offer.

"Not tired." Jake yawns. "School ... lunch with me ..." he mumbles bits and pieces as he finally gives in, and his body goes limp with sleep.

"I'll tuck him in if you have lunch with him tomorrow," Tripp says softly, rounding the table to take his son from my arms.

Jake doesn't move a muscle in the transfer, and again, I marvel at how Tripp slides seamlessly out of operator mode and right into dad mode.

I push back my chair and gather the dessert plates, helping Chloe load up the dishwasher. "Thank you. This was perfect."

"Not perfect enough to stay with us though?" she challenges.

"Jesus, Chloe." I huff out a laugh. "Give me a break. I've had him nonstop for the past six months. You all need to reconnect, and I need to do the bachelor thing." I close the dishwasher and drain the last of my beer. "But tell me about lunch. How do I do this shit? I have no clue."

Chloe gives me all the details on where to go, when to be there, and what to bring. She stops just shy of telling me to make good choices and use my manners or I might get sent to the principal's office as Tripp stalks silently into the room.

With his son tucked away for the night, the air between him and his wife changes, charged with electricity, and without a doubt, it is time for me to leave. Tripp tosses me my truck keys and promises to take care of returning the rental car in the morning, practically shoving me out the door.

This is why I need to give them some space. They need to complete the fall into normalcy. My friends are incredibly welcoming, inviting me into their home and their lives, but I refuse to be *that* guy. They need alone time, and I find what I'm after—a clean hotel, a bottle of Don Julio 1942 tequila, and room service.

And, though I'm sure as shit not looking for Mrs. Right, I can at least venture out and maybe enjoy the company of Miss Right Now.

3

Kate

I SHOULDN'T HAVE FAVORITES in class. Not supposed to give one kiddo more chances than any other to get his poop in a group. Normally, I'm pretty fair, but Jake Triplett has burrowed his little self into my heart in a way that I couldn't fight, and now, the little shit is acting six different kinds of crazy. Bouncing around the room, talking a mile a minute, generally disrupting the entire class. And it doesn't matter how much patience I have with these littles; I can't lose control of twenty five-year-olds and expect to walk out of here alive today. Mob mentality applies.

"Jake, please take your seat. It will make my heart sad if I have to ask you to move your pin, friend," I sternly tell him. Well, as sternly as I can because, no matter what I tell myself, this little guy is my damn favorite.

"But, Miss Beard, my uncle Jack is a soldier and he's a hero like my dad and he's here," Jake shares as loudly as he dares, completely ignoring the warning tone in my voice. "He was at my house last night and had dinner with me and my mom and my dad, and he told me about the big desert and did you know they don't get play time? He doesn't get to play in the sand at all even though he's there all the time with my dad. And-and-and they don't even like going to the beach anymore; isn't that weird? And—"

I can't. I just can't.

"Jake." I lower my voice and raise my brows, cutting him off before he has a chance to really kick it into high gear. "I'm sorry, but you need to move your pin and take your seat."

The shock that registers across his sweet little-boy features about breaks my heart. It's like a personal affront that I asked him to move his little Jake-looking clothespin off the green dot and onto the yellow one. Any other kid, and I'd have probably already had him on orange and well on his way to the dreaded red dot, followed by a note home to his parents. But I adore this kid, and he is normally so damn sweet and minds so well.

"But, Miss Beard—"

"Jake, move your pin, please, and have a seat," I repeat.

My heart fissures as his little face falls, tears gathering in the corner of his big brown eyes as he does the walk of shame to the pin board.

"Yes, ma'am. I'm sorry." He sniffs. With all the solemnity that this very dire situation deserves, Jake moves his pin to yellow.

Head bent and shoulders slumped, he walks back to his seat and gets to work. I feel like I've sent him off to his doom. With his tongue out and curled around his upper lip, pencil clutched in his chubby little hand, brows pulled tight in concentration, he traces his letters, practicing the skill, though he's probably one of my most advanced students.

Before long, Jake's wiggling in his seat, checking the clock over the door, sneaking surreptitious glances at me. I shake my head and jot a quick note to myself to check in with his mama and make sure there's nothing else going on in his little world that has him so out of sorts.

AFTER HANDING MY CLASS off to the lunchroom monitor, I hightail it to the teachers' lounge and grab my lunch from the fridge. Thank God my roommate, Gracyn, went food shopping this week. She's an amazing friend but a real shitty cook; she could barely tell you what the inside of a grocery store looks like. She did good this time though.

I pull the big roast beef on rye out of my paisley-printed lunch bag and peel back the wrapping. Crisp lettuce and tangy onion give each bite a perfect crunch, and the flavors positively burst in my mouth. Slathered with cheesy Parmesan mayo and bright red tomato, this sandwich is nothing short of heaven. I wash down each bite with a hit of water, focused on getting the food in my belly as fast as I can.

"The hell, Kate? Where's the fire?" my fellow kinder-garten teacher Annie asks. She plops down at the table next to me and empties her own bag of goodies.

Teaching the youth of America to properly form their

letters is hard work; we tend to take our food quite seriously.

Speaking around another mouthful, I answer, "Something's up with Jake, and I don't want him to get in trouble in the lunchroom. He's a frickin' spaz today, and Martha'll send him to the office if I'm not there."

Martha is the elementary school equivalent of a SWAT team. She runs a tight ship, and nobody messes with that.

Chew, swallow, gulp of water, and another huge bite. My sandwich is almost done, and I pray that I have a mint in my bag for later because this onion is seriously strong.

"You've got it bad for that little boy, don't you? What happened to not having a favorite this year?" Annie teases.

Shrugging, I shove the last bite in my mouth and chew furiously before responding, "What can I do? His daddy's gone a lot, and he just needs a little extra patience right now. I'll talk to his mama, but he just ... I don't know."

"Doesn't hurt that he's cute as a button either."

"Who? Jake or his daddy? Have you met Mr. Triplett?" I ask, chucking my trash in the can.

"I haven't, but I bet the apple didn't fall far from that tree. And who knows, maybe that uncle Jake's always talking about is single," Annie tosses over her shoulder as I leave the oasis and fast-walk down the hall to my kiddos.

It's not unusual for me to pop in and check on my class, but I startle Martha, laying a hand on her back as she's gunning for my class table.

"Little Mr. Triplett needs a write-up to the office, Miss Beard. In fact, I was just about to take him down there and get things back in order here," she huffs at me.

"Yeah, Jake's had a rough morning, but let's give him a hot minute and just see if he can pull himself out of whatever this is. What's he been doing?" I ask, glancing over my shoulder toward the table reserved for my kids.

Hot damn.

That is most definitely not one of my kindergartners.

Making a show of fanning myself, I tease, "Miss Martha, you sure you don't just want to go over there and flirt with that fine specimen of man sitting next to Jake?" *Because, holy fuck, is he ever?*

Martha pauses and looks at the tall man folded awkwardly into the bench-and-table combo that perfectly fits our smallest students. "Miss Beard," she says exasperatedly, "I'm old enough to be his mother." She flutters her hand at her throat, clutching at the neck of the candy-cane-printed turtleneck that complements her black sweater vest, which has presents and bows appliquéd festively down the front.

"Doesn't mean you can't look." I hit her with a wink and lean in conspiratorially. "You calling dibs on him? Or can I go see what's got Jake all riled up?"

"Dear Lord, you're just terrible," she mutters. "But, since you're here, I'll let you deal with your class issues. I see a potential situation that needs to be handled with that long-term substitute's class." And, with that, Martha scurries off, leaving me to my musings.

The man sitting smack-dab in the middle of the bench is obviously a source of great interest to my kids. Jake alternates between sitting so close to the man that a piece of tissue paper would feel squished and standing, holding court with his tall, muscly friend. Probably his dad. He did mention that his father was home earlier. He's got all the telltale patience of a father visiting his excited kiddo at school. Helping each child open whatever container or snack bag they hand him. Chatting with each of them in turn.

Chloe Triplett is a very lucky woman if that man is warming her bed at night—when he's in town anyway. His broad shoulders test the tensile strength of the fabric of his plaid shirt, molding almost poetically around a muscular back, tapering in that perfect V to a well-formed ass.

God, forgive me for lusting after my student's father, please and thank you, I pray silently.

Closely cropped dark brown hair fades into maybe two-day scruff that peppers a strong jawline. Plump lips hitch up when the question of the moment is interrupted by Amelia telling him he's got pretty eyes.

His shoulders shake ever so slightly as he rumbles out a, "Thank you, and so do you."

Be still my heart.

I take a deep breath as I approach the table, pushing aside any and all of those lustful thoughts that might still be floating around me like fireflies on a hot summer night. "Jake, can you have a seat, please?" I rest a hand on his shoulder, giving him a little clue about which direction he needs to make his body go.

"Hey, sorry. Hope I'm not causing any trouble." The man turns and thrusts his hand in my direction, trying to stand.

Bless his heart for trying to have manners, but that

table has a hold on him, and I'm not quite sure it's ever going to let him go. I wouldn't.

"Not at all. Actually, I'm thrilled to meet you, Mr. Triplett. Jake has been talking about you nonstop. Thank you for your service." I smile and nod my head before slipping my hand into his, and no matter how wrong it is, my heart does an extra little dance when our hands connect. *All the good ones are taken.*

"That's not my dad," Jake says, screwing up his face at me like I'm an idiot. "That's my uncle Jack, Miss Beard. Uncle Jack, didn't I tell you she was pretty? I did, right?"

Electricity jumps along my spine as a smile spreads across this man's beautifully tanned face. Blue eyes flecked with green and gold stay trained on my muddy browns, not breaking eye contact, even as his smile wrinkles and creases the skin at the corners of his eyes.

"You did, my man. You absolutely did. I'm at a disadvantage here, Miss Beard. I seem to be trapped and can't stand to properly introduce myself." He's still got my hand firmly clasped in his, deep golden-brown skin wrapped solidly around my winter-paled hand. "Wyatt Jackson. Uncle Jack to this guy." He nods toward Jake. "It is an absolute pleasure to meet you, ma'am."

If I were a less jaded woman, I'd swoon. But I'm not, and this slick soldier is too smooth, too good-looking, and probably just like all the other assholes out there. I need to shake this off and get myself together. Somehow, it was safer to lust after Jake's very happily married dad. His apparently single and possibly interested uncle is dangerously enticing.

I smile politely and pull my hand from his warm grip, his palm rough and callused, his hold strong. "Thank you for visiting with us today, Mr. Jackson. Jake speaks very highly of you," I tell him.

"As he does of you." He winks a golden-greenish blue eye at me "Every time we talk, right, buddy?"

Jake wiggles out of his seat and bounces in front of me. "Can Uncle Jack come to class? Can I show him my seat and my cubby and all of my pictures? Can I, please?"

"Chill, bud. You're bouncing like a bunny," I tell him through a chuckle. "We've got a busy afternoon—"

"Please, Miss Beard. Please? I promise I'll be good the rest of the day. I promise," Jake begs.

Maybe I could resist his folded hands and the puppy-dog eyes on a normal day, but this is special. Jake's been talking about his dad and uncle coming home forever, and as rocky as the morning was, the afternoon won't be any better if I say no to this.

Pick your battles, Kate.

"All right, but you need to pinkie promise me that you're going to calm yourself down." I hold out my right pinkie to Jake, and he carefully wraps his around mine and places his other hand over his heart.

"I promise, and soldiers never break their promises, right?" He looks to his uncle and returns the nod of acknowledgment he gets.

"Without a doubt." That deep, gravelly voice sends sparks down my spine.

4

Jack

JAKE CLUTCHES MY HAND as we walk down the hallway, our free pointer fingers resting tightly against sealed lips. Not a sound aside from the slap of rubber soles against the shiny linoleum—that, and the click of Miss Beard's heels. Those shiny black heels lead up to legs that could only have been created by God himself on his most inspired day in heaven. And that ass. Is that sway normal for a kindergarten teacher? Thank Christ she's not teaching middle school; boys would be throwing 'bows, trying to gain just the tiniest bit of her attention. Hell, I'd fucking throw down just for the chance to hold her hand again.

How many times can I get away with shaking her hand before I solidly enter creep territory?

"Okay, boys and girls, please put your lunch bags away and take a seat on the floor. You may bring your mat or snuggle buddy if you want," the hot teacher says. Her voice is like silk, smooth and calming with just a hint of a Southern accent.

I'm not a linguist, but I learned early on that it pays to pay attention, picking apart accents and speech patterns. The more I can piece together about people when I meet them, the better my life tends to be.

"Uncle Jack doesn't have a mat or snuggle buggle," Jake calls as he darts to his cubby. "But we can share. I'll use my coat, and you can use my dino mat." The kid is dragging half of the coat closet with him.

"Jake, maybe your uncle would like to sit up front and read to us today?" Teach raises her eyebrow at me.

Questioning me? Daring me? I'm not sure, but I am sure as fuck getting lost in the way her eyes sparkle at me.

I stalk to the fluffy pink chair at the front of the classroom, my very best panty-melting smile on my face. Being the teacher's pet right about now sounds like an excellent way to spend a day. Maybe more than a day while I'm in town. I sure as shit don't remember any of my teachers filling out a tight skirt like she does.

"I'd be honored to read today." I throw her a wink and settle myself into the frilly deep-pink chair. It might be petite and delicate, but at least it's adult-sized, not like the minuscule chairs dotting the rest of the room.

Miss Beard approaches me from behind, and I force myself not to react like I'm in the field. Multiple tours in the devil's sandbox have made me a little jumpy about not having my six covered. Dropping a sparkly purple purse and a book into my lap, she explains what we're reading today. She stands to my right and leans into the side of the princess chair I'm planted in, her hip jutting dangerously close to the side of my head. I grip the shiny purse in my hand, the plastic groaning under the pressure as I force myself to keep my hands firmly and safely on my lap. The temptation to reach back and trail a finger up the back of her curvy calf, across the back of her knee, and up that thigh is almost overwhelming. But I'm disciplined; I've had that shit beaten into me, hazed and burned into my very being.

A rhythmic snapping draws my attention from inappropriate thoughts, and with that subtle little noise, the kids all find their spots on the floor in a semicircle around me.

Softly, melodically, Miss Beard praises the group, "Thank you for being such good listeners. Let's take just a moment to say thank you to Jake's special guest for taking time to read with us today."

A chorus of, "Thank you," jumbles into a mix of, "friend," and, "Uncle Jack."

I've seen soldiers who don't follow direct orders half as well as these little kids do with nothing more than a kind voice and some gentle prodding. How much of that can be attributed to the woman who's got them for the majority of their waking hours each day? Hell, after just a handful of minutes with her, I'm ready to fall in line and do whatever she wants.

I steal a glance at the delicate hand propped on her left hip—right where I almost can't miss it. I mean, I *can't* miss it. Relief floods me when I see that her hand is completely unadorned. No rings. None glinting on the hand in the air, reaching to turn on a lamp resting on the edge of her desk. That's a damn good sign for me. Surely, she felt that surge when we shook hands earlier. For fuck's sake, I didn't want to let go.

She saunters across the room, blonde waves bouncing, to turn off the overhead light, casting the room in a soft glow, and with a collective sigh, the kids settle in for story time.

I'm not going to lie. The purple purse story doesn't really hold anyone's interest. Before long, heads are nodding, eyes are closing, and there's complete and utter silence. I close the book and set it on the bookshelf next to me with the purse and silently push myself up out of the chair. There, in the shadows, is a stunning beauty, lit by a desk lamp and the glow of her laptop.

"Is this normal, or did I bore them to death?" I whisper.

"This is a golden miracle, and we don't look a gift horse in the mouth," she says softly, her accent weaving its way around the words. "I love each and every one of them, but peace is peace, and I need it today. Thank you."

She looks around the room, taking stock of the lax, snoozing bodies strewed across the floor. Gracefully standing, she motions for me to follow her, and we slip out into the hall, the door barely cracked behind us.

"Seriously, thank you. Some days are rougher than others, and if I'm being honest, I think they all need the break. Being five is hard work." She smiles, really smiles for the first time since I met her, and it's breathtaking.

"Shit, I'm sorry. Was it me, do you think? Jake's got a

tendency to get himself worked up, and he takes the rest of the room along for the ride."

Her hand darts out, landing on my arm, her intent to soothe my worry away. But with her movement comes a waft of perfume, and the effect is the absolute opposite of what is good for either of us in this moment. Soft and buttery like whipped cream, fresh but not overly sweet, her scent is nothing short of heady and intoxicating in the very best way.

"Not at all, and please watch your words," she says, pinning me with a stern teacher look. "I think it has more to do with the phase of the moon or the fact that Christmas break is looming around the corner."

I place my hand on top of hers, holding it in place. "Miss Beard, thank you for all that you do for Jake. People don't usually get how hard it is on those left behind by deployments. You've made a huge impression on him."

Her smile takes on a hint of shyness.

"I'd like to thank you properly. Can I buy you a drink? Take you out to dinner?"

"That's sweet of you, but no." She's still relaxed, not pulling away.

"Just no?" I lean in, testing her commitment to that response.

"Yes. A simple no. Perhaps a *no, thank you* would be more polite." She gives my forearm a little squeeze and pulls her hand away.

"May I ask why?" Without conscious thought, I widen my stance and fold my arms across my chest, slipping into my standard pose when a soldier gives me a bullshit answer that I don't like.

"You may."

Sighing, I drop my chin to my chest before meeting her eye again. "Why did you refuse an offer for a lovely dinner out?"

"Professionalism. Do they have that in the Navy?"

"Army, Special Forces. SEALs just fucking write books. I actually do work," I respond automatically, busting on my Naval counterparts.

Given the same situation, guys from the other services all do the same thing, but when shit goes down, there is nothing but mad respect.

Her head snaps back, eyes blinking wildly, making her lashes flutter. "Same difference, and I asked you to watch your language," she scoffs, glaring. "I just don't think it's right to see my students' people socially. It would raise questions of impropriety, but thank you anyway."

My lips pull up on just one side in a smirk that has never failed me. I lean in, crowding her space just a little—not enough to scare her off because, let's face it, the last thing I want to do is give her any reason to refuse me. "I'm not related to Jake. He's my best friend's kid, and while I think of them as family, we're not a blood relation."

"And yet, my student calls you Uncle Jack, thus the need to maintain distance. So, *no*, but thank you." She gives my in-charge stance right back, feet planted, arms folded, attitude in full swing.

I like it. Fuck that, I like it a lot that she's a little cocksure and sassy. Color me intrigued.

"True. But I can assure you, I have sufficient security clearance to keep this on the down low if that's what you need ..." I taper off, waiting.

And waiting.

Nothing.

This chick has her shit locked down tight, making me the first to break. "Christ, will you at least tell me your name, or do I have to keep calling you Miss Beard?"

The attitude on this one, seriously fucking hot.

She screws up her mouth so that her plump peach lips are twisted up, the right side of them getting downright abused by her pearly white teeth. "Doesn't matter if y'all are actually related, the answer is still no. And you keep pushin', we're gonna ramp that no right on up to a hell naw, ya hear? And my name is Katelyn Hays Beard. I'll allow Kate, should we happen to run into each other outside of school, but within these walls and with Jake, I expect you to respect my professional relationship with your nephew and his family, referring to me as Miss Beard. There's more to family than just blood."

Yeah. Her Southern roots are showing big-time, and I definitely like ruffling those feathers.

"Right. I hear you. Thank you for your time today, ma'am." I nod and saunter down the kindergarten hallway like I own the fucking place.

5

Kate

THERE IS NOTHING I need more than dinner and a handful of drinks to help wash away a week from hell with twenty five-year-olds and a full moon. At least I hope that's what I'm getting up to tonight.

This is the third, maybe fourth time I've gone out with this guy, and while he's not the worst I've found on Tinder, he's sure not winning any awards either. In fact, Dr. Barnes, as he refers to himself, is kind of an asshole. He's got potential to be a lovable one at times, but still. I mean, for the love of God, he's a chiropractor; he can't even hook me up with antibiotics when the sweet little angels in my class lovingly share their damn germs. It's time for him to up his game, but I probably need to cut him loose. After dinner because, to be completely honest, a teacher's salary doesn't go very far, and I really do need a night out to counterbalance this week.

"Yes, I made a reservation," he says, rapping his knuckles on the hostess stand. "My time is valuable. You think I have all the time in the world to stand around, waiting for you to find me a table? I'm a doctor, for God's sake."

"I'm so sorry, Dr. Barnes. Perhaps you can have a drink at the bar while we get your table ready for you?" The poor girl is beyond flustered and falling all over herself to make Matt happy.

Yeah, I refuse to refer to him as a doctor. Maybe I would if he wasn't such an asshole. But he is, so there's that.

I lean on the bar and signal the bartender. "Two shots of Patrón and a margarita. Rocks and salt, please," I order quickly, hoping I can get some liquid calm before the not-a-doctor loses his shit.

As the bartender sets the full shot glasses in front of me, a most delicious smell drifts around me. I check over my shoulder for the source of the clean, spicy scent with a hint of citrus and leather, but no one stands out to me. Downing the shots, one after the other, I slide a wad of cash across the bar and scoot to my left, making room for Matt.

He's fine. At the very least, not visually offensive.

"Can you believe how they treat medical professionals here? Honestly, if I ran my practice like this, I wouldn't have any patients," Matt huffs indignantly. "Did you get a drink, KB? That bartender take care of you?" He's talking to me but looking anywhere but at me.

"I did. What do you need?" I turn and smile at the bartender, hoping he comes right over.

Maybe this was a bad idea. Maybe dinner and drinks aren't worth the time I have to spend with this guy.

"Yeah, I'm gonna need an appletini," Matt calls over my head, doing the douchey bro nod at the sweet man pouring drinks tonight. "And that's on the house since I have to wait for my reservation."

I want to disappear. Usually not offensive just became full asshole.

What self-respecting man drinks appletinis?

None. The answer is not a damn one.

Matt's froufrou girlie drink is placed in front of him with a look that might be classified as heated interest from the bartender.

I catch his eye and give him a quick shake of my head, mouthing, *Don't waste your time.*

Lifting the full glass to his lips, Matt takes a delicate sip and loudly smacks his lips. A move that does not go unnoticed by the bartender despite my warning. Perhaps they're better suited for each other than Matt and I are.

"So I had a new patient today. Fucking hot as shit. Tight body, locked in on clean eating. She was totally a CrossFitter; I could tell. She had these rock-hard thighs and this ass. She's going to need me for a long time coming." He snickers, mumbling, "Come," under his breath like he's saying a naughty word—like the twelve-year-old boy he really is at heart.

Sweet baby Jesus in a manger, this date is going downhill in a hurry. There is not a damn thing I can think of to say. Matt's practically panting over some other chick while he's out with me. When is this shit going to end? I need to find a nice man. One with ethics and morals. One who knows how to treat the woman he's out on a date with. One who refrains from looking for or lusting after his next conquest. Doesn't have to be a forever thing. I just need to know that the apparent unicorn exists.

The front door opens, ushering in a gusty breeze from outside, and that spicy, citrusy scent swirls around me once again. The owner must be somewhere close by. I search the surrounding area, and just as I lock eyes with my favorite student's not-a-real-uncle, Matt's commentary on his better business practices rumbles across the room.

"So, really, I mean, it's only malpractice if they complain, am I right?" Matt's booming, slightly grating voice carries across the sudden lull of conversation in the bar area.

There is no escape. None.

"Dr. Barnes, your table is ready. Would you care to follow me, please?" The hostess smiles politely, indicating the way to the dining room.

Matt rises from the barstool he commandeered for himself, leaving me to stand in three-inch heels. "About time. We've been waiting well over ten minutes."

The more he talks, the more I realize I'm not just not interested; I'm downright embarrassed to be associated with him. Resigned to just get through tonight's dinner and call it quits.

Again.

I can't seem to catch a break with the whole dating

thing since I showed up early to meet my ex, Chance, for dinner and found him pressed up—from hips to lips—kissing on the prettiest boy I had ever seen. Needless to say, I moved out the next day, and the rest has been one dating disaster after another. The only good thing that came out of that day was meeting my roommate, Gracyn George, and her best friend, Lis Rittenhouse. Thank God those girls were all about making friends with a poor, displaced girl from the South.

We're seated at a table by the window, and Matt immediately launches into ordering for both of us. Not a damn thing that I want to eat since the self-proclaimed fitness guru has decided that kale and brussels sprouts are the food of the hour.

I excuse myself as quickly and politely as I can manage, seeking the relative silence of the women's restroom. It strikes me out of nowhere that this is becoming my thing. My date starts going south, and I take off for the sanctity of the restroom—the one place I know the guy won't follow me. I wash my hands, check social media, and waste as much time as I think I can get away with. Maybe our super-healthy, flavorless food will be at the table, waiting, by the time I get back. Doing a quick calculation of how much time I think I can handle spending with Matt Barnes —full-naming him is a fantastic middle ground for me, not too familiar, not at all professional—I push through the restroom door and stop dead in my tracks.

Wyatt Jackson. Standing just like he did outside my classroom earlier today when he was trying his damnedest to look intimidating. Feet shoulder-width apart, arms folded across his broad chest, biceps straining against the confines of his flannel shirt. Waiting. I inhale deeply, readying myself to be just as indignant as I can when the spicy, citrus scent from earlier stops my brain mid-thought. Of course it was him—the source of the scent that calmed me, caught my attention, and yet eluded me in the bar.

"That's the kind of guy you go for?" A smirk pulls at the corner of his mouth.

"What?"

"I got turned down for that asshole who thinks it's perfectly fine to throw a tantrum for a table and talk to his date about the hot woman he met today that he apparently gets to have his hands all over. What does that say about you, Miss Beard?" His smirk grows as he talks.

The hallway seemingly narrows. Or maybe that's just my reaction to being in a confined space with him.

"You teach those kids about respect and honor—yeah, Jake tells me all about class and his favorite teacher every time he's got the opportunity, so I am well aware of what you're instilling in those kids—but you don't have it in yourself to demand the same of the people you date?"

Hot and flustered, I'm not sure what to say. Maybe I should try to push my way through and put some space between us, so I can think. I mean, I just met this man for the first time today, and he's getting all in my business?

"I think you're worth more than you're billing yourself."

He straightens his already-rigid spine, and I can't help but notice the striking form he presents. Confidence rolls off of him, swirling around me, filling the air, but he's not cocky. It's just the unspoken assurance that he's a bigger badass than anyone else in the room.

"Mr. Jackson—"

"If you insist on formalities, it's Captain." His head tilts down ever so slightly as his brows rise up the same amount.

We're just posturing, dancing around each other.

I purse my lips and pull deep at my teacher voice, the voice of calmly rational sternness, but before I can address him further, he relaxes his shoulders and continues, "I'd prefer if we could drop it though. Jack works a whole lot better for me, Kate. And, if I'm completely honest here, I think you should let me take you out. Show you how a gentleman acts on a date. Bet he doesn't open doors or get your chair for you." He nods his head toward the dining room, and a knowing smile spreads across his face.

I'm dumbstruck. He exudes masculinity and control, not sacrificing even an ounce of respect in the course of it though.

"Why? Why do you want to take me out so badly?" I ask hesitantly, not sure that I can handle his response.

"Because you've got the hardest job in the world—hell of a lot harder than mine. You give all you have to those kids, and I think you don't have an inkling of the impact you have on their little lives. Because you exude a confidence that screams sexy and self-assured, but you lower yourself to letting a schmuck like that think he's worthy of your company. It doesn't make sense, and I want to puzzle it apart, figure out why." Uncrossing his arms, he slides his hands into the front pockets of his jeans. And waits.

My brain whirls and swirls. Thoughts bouncing around, not really sticking on any one thing. My breath catches in my lungs as I search for anything intelligent to say. Anything at all.

And all I can seem to come up with is, "Okay."

He nods once, controlled and almost curt, but even that small movement grabs my attention. "Excellent. Give me your number, and I'll call to work out the details—day, time, your address."

I snap out of the trance I somehow slipped into in the haze of his self-assurance. "No," I say, shaking my head.

"No? No what? Not going to allow me to take you out? Or—"

"I'll meet you out, somewhere public." He opens his mouth to protest, but I push on, "I just met you. It would be foolish of me—actually stupid—to give you my address at this point." I wave my hand toward the restaurant's dining room, realizing I've probably been gone way longer than is polite. "He doesn't even have my address yet, and we've gone out several times. Not all my choices are bad ones. You could be a murderer or something."

He huffs out a laugh and says, "Smart girl. I feel a little better, knowing you're not relying on that douche to get you home safely. Not sure he can hold his liquor. Fucking appletini? What is he, trying out for a remake of *Scrubs* or something?"

"Right? Who drinks those?"

The remaining tension drains out of his body, his stance much more relaxed now. I dig through my bag, looking for a pen and a scrap of paper. Normally, I have

Post-it Notes, a full set of colored pens, and highlighters of all shades in my purse, but I opted to leave my Mary Poppins bag at home tonight, and there is nothing in my clutch to jot my number on.

"Just text yourself from mine."

This would be a fantastic time to let my sass shine, but I'm coming up short, so I just text my name.

He slightly shakes his head and lets out a determined breath. "I know it's presumptuous, but will you ... will you let me know that you've gotten home safe tonight? After dinner?"

I smile, laughing softly at his request. "That is pretty presumptuous. I'll be fine, but I'll talk to you soon," I say, slipping past him to return to my very last date with Dr. Barnes.

If this goes nowhere in the long run and Mr. Right remains elusive, Jack has a point. I deserve more in my evenings ... even if the star is strictly Mr. Right Now.

6

Jack

No MATTER HOW MANY times I check, my phone remains idle. Silent. Dark. A useless piece of shit.

It was a toss-up last night as I sat at the bar, finishing my dinner, on whether to be a creep and follow Kate to make sure she got home okay or to sit tight and be a reasonable human being. I went with reasonable and rational, sending a quick text to the number she'd entered, hoping it was really hers and not a bullshit fake. I have nothing to base this shit on—this concern. But it would have taken nothing for her to send me a damn message. Just a quick, *Home. Safe. Here.*

Something.

But, no, I got nothing from her, and that asshole she was with gave me a bad feeling. The voice mail I left this morning has gotten no response either, and that's just pissing me right the fuck off. I offload my bar and step away from the squat rack. The United States Military Academy gym is fairly empty with the cadets in their academic hours, so I take my time. Pop the clips, add another plate to each end, and get my head right. I don't need an injury, just need to work this woman out of my system.

A quick breath progression once the bar is settled across my shoulders, and I get into position. There is no need to waste time with five hundred-plus pounds on my back, so I get straight to it. Squat and up. Squat and up until my last set's done.

Once the bar is stripped and the plates put away, I flip my phone over, and of course, I have a missed call.

"Hey, this is Kate Beard returning your call. I appreciate your offer, but I think I'm going to pass on dinner. Thank you for the offer and enjoy your day." Her message is pert and professional, just like she wanted.

Well, fuck. I pull on a beanie and my jacket, pop my earbuds in, and head out. I hate running. It's mindless and stupid, absolutely fucking pointless, but I take off through town, hoping that the monotony will clear my head and burn off some of the disappointment. It's not like I've never been turned down before—this is not an ego thing—but she's cute. Sassy. Hell, who wouldn't want to spend some time with a fuck-hot teacher? Maybe coffee? I should take her out for coffee first, ease into this. I told her I wanted to show her how a gentleman treated a lady, give her a different experience than the ass she was out with last night, so I need to do exactly that.

I push through my last couple of miles and take a quick shower, thinking hard about how to change her mind *again*. Get her to go out with me. And, at the same time, I'm doing a fantastic job in avoiding looking at why this has become a fucking mission.

With a quick stop to grab a few things, I pull into visitor parking ten minutes early because, if I'm not early, I'm late. And I can't stand being late. The buzzer sounds, and the lock clicks open, granting me respite from the cold wind whipping past Beekman Hills Elementary.

"What can I help you with today?" the secretary asks, a smile plastered across her face.

I pull out my identification and hand it across the counter, checking the name on the nameplate. "Mrs. Simpson, I'm here to see Miss Beard. This is her lunch period, correct?"

She studies my military ID, flipping it from front to back. "It is, Captain Jackson. Is she expecting you?" she asks, one hand on her phone.

"I'm afraid not, ma'am. If that's a problem, I'd be happy to leave this for her," I say, placing the to-go bag on the counter. I'd much rather see Kate, but I'm not about to rock the boat at her place of employment.

"Miss Beard, you have a package in the front office. Can you swing on by after your lunch drop-off?" Mrs. Simpson quips, giving me a sly wink. "No, I'm sure you'll want to tend to this before you eat. Yes, okay. See you in a bit." Ending the call, she turns to me and says, "She'll be right up, if you'd like to take a seat. And thank you for your service."

I thank her and sit by the window, waiting patiently. Hopefully, this won't be an imposition, though Chloe assured me that it's cool to stop by the school. I might have mentioned wanting to drop a cupcake by for Jake during his lunchtime. It's not a lie, not really. There's a mini cupcake in the bag—his favorite flavor—along with the hot soup, sandwiches, and full-sized chocolate cupcake for Kate.

"Hey, Jenny. What's my package? I didn't order anything. Oh—"

I stand, drawing her attention. "I brought you lunch." I nod, taking her in from head to toe. A long-sleeved shirt and curve-loving skirt have never looked so damn good. Hell, she's more gorgeous than I remembered.

"Thank you." Kate's brows push together, and her lips purse into a biteable pout. "Are you ... did you want to join me?"

"I'd love to."

Familiar with the process, I sign in on the clipboard and grab my visitor sticker before opening the door for Kate. She slides past and leads me down the hallway to her classroom.

"What are you doing here?" She glances at me over her shoulder as her ass sways seductively with each step. "I left you a message this morning that—"

"I got it. You said dinner was a no-go, so I thought I'd bring you lunch."

"Jack"—she pauses to open her door—"that's not what I meant. I just think it's best to keep things separate—personal and professional, I mean."

I nod slowly, having fully expected some kind of resistance. "Gotcha. Well, there's a treat for Jake in there, so if it makes you feel better, you can give him the lunch as well, but I have a feeling he's not going to appreciate lobster bisque the way you might. Totally up to you though. I just wanted the opportunity to thank you for what I'm sure can feel like a thankless job at times."

I set the bag on the corner of her desk and take a step back to pivot and go. No one likes getting their marching orders, and that's exactly what this is. A dismissal.

I might not agree with her reasoning, but who the fuck am I? And can I blame her? I understand professionalism. Understand keeping things compartmentalized. That's how I get through each tour in the desert because that sandbox is so fucking brutal.

A deep sigh and a muttered, "Shit," hits my back as I reach for the door handle.

I pause, turning slightly to face her while I wait.

"I just don't get it. Why are you such a pain in my ass?" Flustered and with her guard down, Kate's accent is more pronounced.

Alabama maybe?

She shifts her weight, popping her hip out, arms crossed over her chest. Classic defensive position, but the way it pushes her tits up is pretty fucking distracting, and I have to briefly close my eyes to find my focus.

"Kate, what's the issue? That I'm a pain in the ass or that I'm pushing your limits of professionalism? I'd like to get to know you, for you to get to know me. It doesn't have to be a big thing. I'm just here for a couple of weeks. Surely, we can have a drink. Dinner." Watching her bite at her plump red lip, I want to do a hell of a lot more than just eat with her, but dinner and drinks would be a great place to start. "I don't want to make you uncomfortable though, so I won't push this anymore. You say the word, and I'll go, drop it, and leave you be. Consider lunch today a good-faith, humanitarian gesture and nothing more." I shrug, nodding to the bag still packed full of food on the corner of her desk. And, of course, my stomach picks that God-given moment to rumble obnoxiously. "Sorry, I'll just—"

"Stay. Eat with me and ... I don't know. Let me think about the rest of it." She pulls containers from the bag. "It looks like you got enough to feed an army."

Her laughter dances through the air, and that shakes something loose in me, drawing me further into the classroom.

7

Kate

SOMEHOW, JACK BROKE THROUGH my resolve yesterday. Well, he did it with lobster bisque and manners that I didn't think I'd seen used properly since I moved to New York. He's got country manners. And the way he carries himself, completely aware of everything and in control at all times is some kind of sexy. Try as I might, it was damn near impossible to resist him. So, now, we're having dinner.

I run home after school and change into a more date appropriate outfit. *Not a date, just dinner.* And why is this so hard for me? I'm not normally this wishy-washy, but something feels different. Bigger, more intense. I have gone back and forth in my mind a hundred times on dating Jack—having dinner. It's just dinner.

As I apply the finishing touches to my makeup, Gracyn

calls out to me from the kitchen. On a whim, I throw my makeup bag into my big tote along with a few other just-in-case essentials and go check out what has Gracyn yelling for me.

The project supplies I ordered are haphazardly stacked by the front door, so I scoop them up and drop the boxes on the kitchen floor, scaring the crap out of Gracyn in the process. I pull all of the craft supplies out and group them by project before repacking them to take to school while we chat. I could ask my kids' parents to send in bits and pieces, but I like knowing what I've got and that it's ready to go for assembly into the cutest Thanksgiving turkeys ever.

"You want some wine?" Gracyn asks, already grabbing a couple of glasses.

"Couldn't hurt," I tell her. "I have a date—hmm, let's not jinx things. I'm having dinner with someone tonight, but I'm sure the wine will help."

"You're rocking the sexy-librarian thing pretty hard. Who is this guy?" She pours us each a glass of Merlot and leans against the counter. "Another Tinder winner?"

"Nope. And I'm sure it won't amount to anything," I say, avoiding. "Let's concentrate on you for a hot minute though. Things rocky with the rock star?"

She tells me all about their back-and-forth, outlining the what-ifs, and damn if she's not trying to talk herself out of falling in love with him.

I tune back in to her saying, "We've spent next to no time together. What if it's just an illusion and we're not at all compatible?"

"What do you mean? Like, sexually?"

Gracyn about snorts her wine out through her nose, sputtering, "The sex is fine, but what if that's all there is? It's not like we can just date like normal people and then walk away when things go south. He's either in LA or on tour, and I'm stuck here. That doesn't bode well for a normal dating relationship."

"When?" I ignore her look of confusion and carry on, "You said 'when things go south,' not *if*. Are you invested or not? Are you willing to take a risk for real, or are you just playing with him?"

And there it is, folks. The dating disaster handing out relationship advice like I have a damn clue. I can dispense the wisdom, but it never seems to work out for me.

I check the time and drain the last of my wine, handing off my empty glass. "I've gotta shake. I'm meeting Mr. Right Now at the restaurant. Don't wait up. If he plays his cards right, he might get dessert," I toss out, going more for shock value than anything.

But it *has* been a long time, and talking with Gracyn about all the amazing sex she's been having with Gavin has me feeling more than a little frustrated. It's been a long dry spell, and I have a fine man taking me out tonight. One who really won't be around long enough to cause any complications. Maybe I will keep the *O* option open.

I flip my ruby-red velvet coat around my shoulders, waiting for the inevitable.

"Be safe and make good choices," Gracyn calls as I sashay out the door.

· · ·

"How did you end up teaching here? You don't sound like you're originally from the area," Jack asks as the waiter leaves us with our drinks.

I'd have ordered a shot of tequila if I'd known we were getting right to the nasty stuff. Instead, I take a healthy sip of my paloma and laugh. Nothing like jumping into the getting-to-know-you portion of the evening.

"I moved here from Mississippi with my high school sweetheart. Go ahead and laugh; it's fine." *Lord, if Jack thinks that little tidbit is funny, he's in for a treat.* "We'd dated forever, all through school and college, and when he wanted to move closer to Manhattan and the Fashion District, I followed him," I say coyly because the rest of the story is where the real kicker is.

Jack leans back in his chair and sets his drink down without taking a taste. "Fashion? He a model or something?" he asks, stroking the stubble along his jawline that gets thicker every time I see him.

"He was something." *Maybe he'll leave it at that.*

"What happened? He run off with a supermodel?" Finally, Jack decides to take that sip of his drink, but the timing couldn't be worse.

He sputters the *añejo* tequila, choking on it, when I say, "I don't know if he was a model, but I caught Chance with his tongue down a guy's throat outside the restaurant we were meeting at for dinner." I shrug because, really ... what else can I do? The whole thing was ridiculous. "That's how I ended up with my two best friends. Gracyn, my roommate, and Lis kind of felt sorry for me as I slammed tequila at the bar of the bistro. It turned out, Gracyn needed a new roommate since Lissy and her boyfriend were moving in together, and it all just worked out."

Jack sets his napkin down after mopping up his spilled drink and asks, "And the guy? Chance? What the fuck happened there?"

"I moved my shit out of the apartment we shared, and his boyfriend moved in the same day, I think. I see him around every now and then, but I think he does his blessed best to avoid me at all costs."

The waiter comes back, dropping off food and filling our water glasses, giving me a little reprieve from the mess that started my long history of dating disasters.

"So, my mama still hears from his mama, and she just can't seem to understand why I would move all the way up here with her boy and then leave him high and dry, making him take a new roommate he hardly knew at all. I think it's safe to say that Chance hasn't come out to his mama and daddy yet. Lord, I'm not looking forward to going home for Christmas and having to deal with that mess." I tip back my glass and take a bracing gulp.

"Wait, you ... your boyfriend, who you dated forever, is gay? And you had no idea?" Jack's eyebrows can't get any further up on his forehead without him pulling a muscle.

"That's correct," I quip.

He pulls his lips between his teeth, biting back a smile. "And your last name is—"

"Yep."

He folds over, practically face-planting in his dinner, loud laughter rolling out of him.

"My last name is Beard, and I had absolutely no idea

that I was his beard." I set my fork down and wait until Jack's at least marginally under control. "I've heard all the jokes about it, made quite a few at my own expense, but aside from my epic dating failures since then, I'm glad. Can you imagine if I'd have married him? And let's be honest; that's where we were headed. Lawd, he's probably still waiting for me to break it to his mama, but that ain't gonna happen, no sir." I steal a glance at Jack just as he registers my *no sir*.

His pupils darken as his posture changes. Gone is the casual and easygoing air, morphing into something heated. Something passes between us that is decidedly sexual. His shoulders broaden, his back goes ramrod straight, and God help me, his tongue lazily sweeps out, moistening his lower lip.

"Katelyn"—his voice holds a note of bridled tension that settles low in my belly, warmth tingling through me— "I like the way *sir* sounds, spilling off your lips."

"Wyatt"—I place my napkin on the table. I am all but done with dinner, the heat and lust quickly bubbling up all around us—"I will *not* call you sir."

"Fair enough. You wanna stay for dessert?" Jack asks, pushing away from the table, poised to stand.

I lean down and grab my purse from the floor. "I think I'd rather be dessert," I purr quietly, standing with more grace than I thought I could muster. I stalk toward the door of the restaurant. I'm not sure what's changed, but I'm ready to break all the rules.

Jack just might be the unicorn I've been looking for.

Manners and chemistry that sizzles. And, since he's only here for a short time, what could possibly go wrong? It's not like I'm going to fall in love in a few short weeks. Fun, flirting, and maybe a little fucking on the side—it sure as hell won't be forever, but maybe all I need is right now.

THE DOOR TO JACK'S room snicks shut behind us, his fingers wrapped firmly around the belt of my jacket. He slowly tugs me into the room, full of quiet confidence and control. And, if I'm being honest, I'm more than willing to follow him. He spins me, untying my belt as he does, my jacket falling to the floor behind me.

With the patience of a hunter, Jack pulls the pins from my hair, letting the waves tumble down around my shoulders. He deliberately flicks the buttons of my blouse, exposing my heated skin, inch by burning inch.

"Christ, you're fucking gorgeous, Kate." He trails a fingertip across my collarbone and down between my breasts.

My skin pulls tight, pebbling my nipples. And, with clothes flying in every direction, we tumble into a writhing, glorious, passionate heap. Thrusting and moaning until both of us are beyond sated and there is nothing left but to pass out from exhausted bliss.

NOISES, MUFFLED VOICES, PULL me from sleep, and it takes a beat or two of my heart for me to remember where I am.

That, and the hard slab of muscle my hand is resting on. I trace my fingers along the ridges, accentuating V-cut muscles that point to heaven. Fine, they point to Jack's cock, but sweet Jesus, that's close enough to heaven for me. I thanked God more than once, and I swear, I saw angels when he thrust deeper than anyone ever had before.

I wrap my fingers around his cock, gently stroking, feeling the weight of him in my palm. Leaning over, I kiss and lick my way down his body, sliding my hand along his hardening shaft.

"You gonna kiss it or just rile it up?" Jack's voice is gravelly and full of sleep. His question turns to a deep groan as I take him into my mouth, swirling my tongue around his ridge. "*Fuck,*" he hisses as I take him as deep as I dare.

There is nothing good about gagging or puking when giving a blow job. *Nothing.*

"Jesus, Kate, let me ... *ung* ... babe ... oh fuck ..." he groans, reaching for the nightstand, fumbling for his wallet.

I pop his dick from my lips and lick slowly, languorously from his heavy balls to the very tip. And, from there, I just keep going, crawling up his body until I'm straddling him, rubbing up and down his steely length. Never have I had this kind of craving for someone. The way he moved me, played me, owned me was like nothing I have ever experienced.

"Need a condom," he murmurs against my neck, hands firmly grasping my hips.

I agree. We need a gross of them.

"Mmm, out. Used 'em," he tells me while sucking on the dip of my collarbone.

With hands planted firmly on his pecs, I push myself up and off of him. "Two? That's all you had?"

Jack cocks an eyebrow at me, running his hands up and down my thighs.

"It's fine," I say, climbing off him. "I've got backups."

I dig around in my bag and pull out my condom stash. A girl can't be too prepared, no matter how long and bad her dry spell is. I toss one of the packages to him and place the rest on the nightstand. We are so going to need them before this night is done.

"What the hell is this?" Jack asks, holding up the purple foil square, a smirk plastered on his face.

"Protection?"

"You get them from a vending machine or something? Are these a joke?" He pushes himself up until his back's against the headboard. "We use this shit on the barrel of our weapons in the desert. Keeps the sand out, but, babe, this ain't gonna work here."

"It's a condom. What's not gonna work?" I climb on his lap and take the package from him, tearing it open. When I try to apply the condom, it becomes abundantly clear what Jack's trying to get at. It's obviously not what he had in his wallet.

"I don't know whether to be flattered by your enthusiasm or concerned that you've just not been properly serviced."

He has the damn nerve to laugh. I mean, I knew right

away there was more to him than I was used to, but honestly.

"Humble you are not," I say, pulling my bottom lip between my teeth. *This has to work.*

"Can be when it's warranted."

8

Jack

"KATE, BABY, LET ME just throw on some clothes and go ..."

She's trying to kill me. I'm absolutely going to die right here.

"It's fine. I got it. Hang on." She's motivated, seriously motivated. "There," she huffs out, lifting up on her knees and rubbing my head through her folds.

"Kinda tight, Kate," I groan as she slides down until I'm fully seated, balls deep.

Her pussy is nothing short of heaven. All nonessential thoughts scatter from my brain, and all my focus is drawn to this woman and the things she's doing to me. Watching her tits bounce as she rides me is a recipe for premature disaster, and there is no way in hell we're going through putting another pencil-sized wrapper on my junk. I grab hold of her ass and flip us over because, with as good as she feels, I *need* to be in some kind of control.

Slowing things down, I pump my hips and drop down onto my elbows, and I swear on all that is good and holy that some of the pressure dissipates. Maybe it's the workup, maybe the change in angle, but the relief is the sweetest. Suddenly, the torture of getting wrapped becomes worth it, and no matter how much thinking about said torture should dial things back for me, this feels *more*. Infinitely better. I snake my arms under Kate's back, pressing her to me, giving a little extra shove at the end of each thrust, making damn certain I'm bottoming out. Every. Single. Time.

"Lawd-'a'-mercy, Jack ..."

My sentiments exactly.

"Kate ..." I'm not gonna last much longer.

"Close. Oh God, so close ..."

And, like I fucking planned it, I feel her muscles clamp down on me, squeezing, massaging, pushing me right the fuck over the edge. Poetry in motion, we both get racked by waves of ecstasy that I sure as shit have never experienced before in my life.

"Why was that so good?" Kate asks, her words breathy and muffled by my shoulder.

I'm probably on the verge of crushing her, but, for fuck's sake, I saw stars, and I'm not sure I can even move yet. Instead of responding, I grunt and reach deep within myself to thrust into her one last time before pulling out and letting the poor girl breathe.

"It was probably the special prophylactic I provided," she mumbles, arm falling over her eyes.

"Kate?" *Jesus, no. You have got to fucking be kidding me.* "You on the pill? Something?"

"No. Why?" she asks, opening her eyes, trailing them down to my dick. "Oh hell."

There's no denying *why* that felt so good. I sit back on my heels, shaking my head because that prophylactic has become problematic.

"Well, you just busted right through that thing, didn't you?" Her gaze bounces from my cock to my eyes and back again. "Obliterated it. I mean, you just fucked right out the other side …"

"Goddamn it. Not funny, Katelyn," I warn. I don't like the edge in my voice, but this is not good. It goes against everything I've fucking planned for myself. "If you weren't dating pencil-dicked douche bags—"

"Hey now. It's not like you're the only one this affects. Are you even clean? That thing"—she waves at my still-hard dick—"could be diseased for all I know."

"Checked regularly and has never jumped without a parachute. And what about you, huh? I'm not sure I like the odds of Appletini Guy being all that hygienically aware."

She slowly blinks at me, like she's either processing what I said or getting ready to slap me. After several more owl-like blinks, Kate scowls and pushes herself up to sitting, almost nailing me in the junk when she folds her legs Indian style—or whatever the fuck they're calling it in kindergarten these days. "A: no. Just no. He sure as hell was not getting with me. In fact, it's been a lifetime, thank you very much. And B: we just did the deed in the wild. Unprotected. No goalie in the net."

"Yeah? What's that look like? What's my risk factor there?" My heart is pounding, panic threatening to pull me over the edge from kind of an asshole to full-on fucking prick.

She looks completely offended but counts in her head, eyes focusing on the ceiling in concentration. Meanwhile, I try to roll the useless thing off.

"*Your* risks should be okay, cycle-wise, and since you're so damn concerned with me, mine should be the same."

She deserves to be pissed. I might have gone further into prick territory than I thought.

"What are you doing?"

Dying. I'm dying of dick asphyxiation. Strangulation of my schlong. "Trying to get this off. Christ, it's like—"

"A cock ring," she says, snorting. "Is it supposed to be turning that color? Guess I know where the whole eggplant-emoji thing came from because I feel like that's what I'm looking at."

"Jesus fuck, Kate. Can you help me here? Gonna have to cut this shit off." I fall forward, hand on the headboard to brace myself because, really? I think I could pass out right about now. "You got some scissors in that bag?"

She slides off the bed and digs through her tote. "You bet your sweet ass I do," she sasses triumphantly. "Here we go. Turn around for me, darlin'."

I fall to the side and sprawl across the bed, blankets rucked up behind my back. "Hold real still now."

There is no way in hell I could have prepared for what I see coming at my junk. "What the fuck are you doing? You're a goddamn kindergarten teacher. Where are your safety scissors?" I put one hand out to stop her and protectively clutch my really unhappy Mr. Happy with the other.

"What?" she asks, obviously not getting just how sensitive this situation is.

I swear to God, I fight to keep my shit together, staring down at the glinting metal of the biggest pair of granny shears I've seen in ages—since I last visited my granny, to be completely honest.

"No way you're coming at me with those ... those ... weapons of mass destruction." Ain't nobody in the world I trust enough to come at me with that noise. "Hell, you're a hostile with a grudge at this point. No, just hell no."

"Jesus, Jack. What do you want me to do? Call 911? You look a little peaked—"

"Do you have—I don't know—lotion? Coconut oil? Maybe we can grease it up and slide it off?"

Or maybe calling the EMTs really isn't a bad option. I'd never live that shit down if it got back to my team. Holy hell, I can't breathe.

"Here, let's just ..." Her hand glides down my length, coating me in—of course she fucking has coconut oil in that bag. "Hold on. I just need to get a good grip." She snickers as her fingers slide over the ring of death, not gaining any purchase. "Um ... wow. That, uh, might have been—"

"Counterproductive," I finish, running through baseball stats, trying to think of my sweet granny without actually thinking of her while my cock gets impossibly harder. "Stop. Just ... stop stroking me. Oh my fucking God."

I feel bad for about a hot minute when she jumps back from me, hands up. Her lip taking some serious abuse between her teeth. But then the panic really starts setting in. I can't think.

Of course I can't think. There's no blood flow to my thinking brain.

"Shower? Cold water? Um ... oh," Kate exclaims as she jumps up, grabbing the hotel robe from the back of the bathroom door. Tying it around her, she bolts out the door with the ice bucket and a room key.

Bracing myself, I limp into the bathroom, holding on to the walls the whole way. The last thing I need is to actually trip and fall on this thing. I'm not sure if it'd break in half or put an indentation in the concrete floor.

Deep, cleansing breaths.

Need to clear my mind.

It doesn't look good, not that a raging, strangled purple —*it's fucking turning purple*—dick is gonna look good in any light, but in the harsh light of the hotel bathroom, things don't look good at all. Veins are popping out like it's their fucking job. Slowly, carefully, I attempt to pick at the band of latex that is squeezing the lifeblood out of me.

My God, I think I really could die from this.

I should have cut my nails. They look like fucking talons ready to rip my dick to shreds. *What if ... what if my fingernail pierces one of the veins in my dick? Could I bleed out from that? For the love of fucks, I have got to get this thing off of my dick before I die. Or pass out. Or die.*

Desperate times. I grab hold and squeeze my base with everything I have, and the damn death ring slides. Just a little. Just enough to give me some hope.

The door swings open, and I don't even care that my ass and angry purple peen are on display for anyone who might be passing by.

"I got some ice. Let me just tie a knot in this. Holy, oh my Jesus, did your thing get bigger?" More snorting that erupts into giggles.

Pretty sure this is the least humorous thing I've ever experienced. Now, if I were hearing the tale from one of my soldiers, different story. I'd be laughing my ass off. And *thing*? She needs to pay some damn respect to my poor, suffering schlong. This situation is so bad.

"What are you ... did you get it to move?" Kate asks, reaching her ice-cold hand out, spilling the ice down my front.

Cock. Balls. All of it is fucking freezing and engorged now. Surely, I'll die soon and just be put out of my misery.

I suck air in through my teeth and glare at her. "Don't." I have never needed freedom like I do at this moment in time. Pulling from my untapped reserves of strength, I repeat my process.

Breathe. Grip. Squeeze. Slide.
Breathe. Grip. Squeeze. Slide.
Breathe. Grip. Squeeze. Slide.

And, by some miracle, the thing slides off, and my dick is free. Finally free. Relief floods me as I sink to the floor, the offending ring of latex discarded to the tiles.

"You okay?" Kate asks softly.

All I can do is nod, my hand gently cupping my cock. Christ, it hurts.

"What can I do?" All signs of snarkiness and sass are gone, and she gently rests a hand on my arm. "Want that shower?"

"Yeah, I think I do." I stand slowly, appreciating my newfound freedom.

Kate leans into the shower, getting the water going, adjusting the temperature until it's just right. Biting her lip, she looks over her shoulder at me, eyes soft and caressing. She stands back and gestures to the pounding water, steam filling the small bathroom. I step under the spray, eyes closed while the warm water washes over me, still clutching my junk. It's like I'm afraid to let it go. I almost lost it tonight, and I really am kind of attached, you know?

I startle and pop my lids up when I feel Kate's hand slide down my arm, gently prying my hand from its protective position.

"Let me see, Jack. Move your hand."

I move it, but don't dare to look until I hear her gasp. *Sweet mother of God, can it be that bad?* I squint one eye closed and look down. Down to where Kate is on her knees in front of me, my bruised dick dangerously close to her lips.

"Does it hurt?" she murmurs, pressing her lips to the tip.

"Mmhmm."

"You think you'll be okay?" Her tongue darts out, licking into the slit.

A groan escapes me as I nod my damn head, watching the show play out before me.

"I'm so sorry," she whispers. "Will you forgive me if I kiss it, make it better?"

My hand slaps the tiled wall in front of me as I fall forward, bracing myself. And, by the time her lips hit the bruised ring around my cock, the tip pushing against the back of her throat, any and all transgressions have been forgiven and forgotten.

"Darlin', if your BJ game is that strong, you're gonna have some bruised knees."

And, as good as I thought it felt with her plump lips wrapped around me, when a laugh rumbles out of her, vibrations slamming down my shaft, I'm almost willing to walk through that fire again.

9

Kate

DAMN MY SHIT LUCK. Murphy and his law have nothing on me because, when I finally meet a guy, a man, who checks all the boxes, it turns out, he's only here for a hot minute. Or a cold month, but whatever.

Tall? Check.

Body? Check.

Manners? Check.

Decidedly straight? All the damn check marks for that one.

And leaving.

I rush through my thankfully minimal end-of-day tasks—wiping off desks, stacking chairs, and putting my room in order. I check my lesson plans and make sure all the supplies are organized for my substitute because I need a long weekend away. Pretty sure I can count on one hand the number of times I've called in or arranged for a sub since I've been teaching, and all of those have been for real-life, actual illnesses. Let's face it; kindergartners are cesspools of germs and have learned the art of sharing those germs like it's the most valuable lesson going. But today, this weekend? I'm out of here.

Jack's time here is coming to an end—his deployment fast approaching—so when he asked if I wanted to get away for a couple of days, go up to the mountains for a long weekend, I jumped at that chance. Hopped, skipped, and jumped. There might have even been a little twirl in there, but I'll neither confirm nor deny that tidbit.

I packed my bag before work today, so that I have nothing more to do than go home and change my clothes. The fifteen-minute drive seems to take far longer, and after sliding my car into a parking spot, I run up the stairs to find a tall, yummy man leaning against the window outside my apartment. Long denim-clad legs casually crossed at the ankles, Sherpa-lined barn coat, unbuttoned to reveal his charcoal-gray thermal. Dark scruff thickening into a beard. *Dear God in heaven, this man is the stuff of dreams.*

"Hey." I smile, stuffing my key into the lock. "I won't be but a quick minute. I just need to change and grab my bag." I peek over my shoulder and startle when he's right there behind me. "Lord, how do you do that? You scared the shit outta me."

"Long, painful lessons and years of practice. Moving silently is a job requirement, and Jake's dad beat the lessons home," he says, holding the door wide open for me.

I set my tote by the door and unload my lunch bag in the kitchen before scurrying down the hall to my bedroom. "Be right out," I toss over my shoulder and about bounce off the doorframe because something about Jack in my space has me spinning and off-balance in the very best way.

"Need any help?" Jack calls from the living room.

I pull a sweater over my head and twist my hair into a low knot. "Thanks, but pretty sure I can handle it," I answer, grabbing the handle of my roller case. "All set. You ready to go?"

"Yes, ma'am," he says, collapsing the handle and lifting my bag.

With my jacket over my arm, I grab my big tote, and out the door we go.

"You have everything good to go at school?" Jack places his hand low on my back as we make our way out of the building.

"I do. Projects are lined up for tomorrow, directions have been spelled out, and an emergency backup plan is ready to go. Lord, I can't believe it's almost Christmas break."

I pause on the street, not sure which way we're headed. Lights flash a short way down the block, and Jack steers me toward a behemoth truck parallel parked impossibly perfect. Having grown up in the Deep South, I am not unfamiliar with boys and their toys. Big trucks make up for small *personalities*, but I know for a fact that Jack is not lacking—anywhere. He opens the passenger door and hands me up into the creamy black leather seat. He shuts me in, deposits my case in the back seat, and rounds the back of the truck before swinging himself behind the wheel.

The engine rumbles to life, and I can't help the snort that escapes in a most undignified manner. I'd deny that it was even me if I thought I could get away with it.

"What's so funny?" Jack asks while maneuvering the huge dark gray truck out into the street. He pulls his seat belt across his broad chest, clicking it into place. Shifting, he pulls his phone from the front pocket of his jeans and hands it off to me. "It should be connected, so just pick a playlist or whatever. But tell me what's so funny."

"Not a thing. Just ... could you have found a bigger truck? I know you're not overcompensating or anything." I scroll through his music app, looking for something, anything that's not R & B or metal.

"You giving me a hard time about my ride?" He smirks, raising a brow. Merging smoothly, Jack slides onto the interstate and heads north toward the Catskill Mountains.

Finally settling on a list, I pick some music—a little bit indie, a touch of alternative, perfect road-tripping tunes. "I would never consider busting on your wheels, but really, this is huge." I can't miss the cocky grin that spreads across his face.

"You like how big it is, sweet cheeks?" He hits me with a roguish grin that makes my insides turn hot and fluttery. "Grew up on a ranch in Montana. Big trucks are all I know. Hauling cattle, moving hay—gotta have size and power to get the job done."

I laugh at his ridiculous play on words and ask, "A ranch? Why'd you leave? That sounds like heaven."

"Mmhmm," he hums. "Hard work that never ends. No vacation, and the hours are shit."

"How's the Army any different?"

Jack glances at me before changing lanes and passing a slow-moving line of cars. "The scenery changes in the Army. Haven't you heard? We get to travel the world."

"You refer to it as *the sandbox*," I say, turning toward him. "I love the beach as much as any good Southern girl, but how can you tell me the scenery in the desert is better than snow-capped mountains in Montana?"

I turn down the music, not wanting to be distracted from our conversation because, right now, there is something else going on with his tone—anger, melancholy. I thought he loved his job, but I'm wondering if I got things wrong.

Jack stares out the windshield, one hand resting casually over the steering wheel while the other scrapes across the light beard covering his cheeks. Silence stretches between us, so thick that I'm not sure if it might be best to change the subject entirely or just let it go. Let him brood and stew over on his side of this ridiculous small-dick mobile.

"I needed to leave. The *scenery* in my town was working hard to tie me down and suffocate me. I had one shot at getting a college education, and the only way for that to happen was for it to be fully funded and be in the name of service to our country. And the farther from home, the better," Jack says, his voice eerily calm and low.

"You were running."

"I was. Not afraid of going back, I'm an entirely different person now. But, at the time, I needed to go."

The finality of his statement leaves no room for doubt that the discussion is done. Obviously, this is a sensitive subject to him, and it's not like this thing with us is going anywhere other than the mountains. This is not a relationship, just a between-deployment hookup for him and a recalibration for me. A reminder that there are good guys out there. Men with manners and honest intent. He's been perfectly candid about what this is and what to expect when his respite ends. He'll go; I'll stay. End of story. The end of our story anyway.

We exit the highway and wind along mountain roads, slowing to pass through small towns. Snow piled high on either side of the road.

"You, uh ..." Jack clears his throat, breaking the silence that has accompanied us for most of the drive. "You want to stop and get a bite to eat before we head to the cabin?"

"I could eat." Turning toward him, I wedge myself into the corner where the seat meets the door. "I'm sorry if I touched on stuff you didn't want to get into, but is this going to be awkward now?"

"Don't want it to be. I should be the one apologizing, not you," Jack says, pulling up to a small Italian restaurant. He puts the truck in park but leaves the engine and heater running. "Look, I love my family, and I love Montana. Ranch life made me who I am, but I wanted more. My mom and dad have never left the state; they hardly even leave the ranch. They had no idea I went through the

69

application process to West Point. I didn't tell them until I was accepted and everything was in place. And then I left." Finally, he turns his head, meeting my gaze. "Let's go in. We can talk more over dinner, okay?" His eyes are pinched at the corners, a cross between pleading and pain.

I purse my lips and nod. "'Kay, or we can just fill our bellies and go snuggle into the cabin and pray for a snow storm."

He relaxes, and the corner of his mouth lifts into a smirk. "I like that. Hang on," he says as he hops out of the truck and comes around to my side. Instead of just holding the door, Jack steps into my space, offering his hands.

"I'm perfectly capable of landing my dismount," I tell him, pivoting and sliding out of the mile-high truck.

"You are, but maybe I wanted my hands on you a little. Get things back on track before we go carb-load for the marathon later."

He crowds my space, running his hands around to my ass, pressing me to him. Teasing, the promise of orgasms hanging in the air. Because this is strictly physical. Here and now. This weekend and maybe one more, and then he'll be gone again. Nothing but a memory that brings a smile to my face and makes my vibrator a woefully inadequate substitute.

"Let's do this thing then." I push my way past him and pat his firm ass as I go.

Jack's chuckle floats behind me as he closes and locks the truck. His hand settles low on my back just as I reach the door, and he steps aside, allowing me to go first.

"Two, please," he tells the hostess, and we're seated

right away at a small table in front of the window, looking out over Main Street of the quaint little town.

"Wine, Kate?"

I nod, and he turns to the hostess before she has a chance to scurry off back to her station.

"A bottle of Chianti, please, and calamari while we decide. Thank you."

The table is covered with an old-school red-and-white-checkered cloth, the dim glow of a candle dancing in the minimal space between us. Our knees brush with each shift as we peel off our coats and settle them on the backs of chairs.

"Your *vino*?" a heavily accented voice asks. White apron, black dress, and the swish of nylon stockings, a short woman approaches our table. Her black hair is pulled back into a severe-looking bun low on her head. She splashes bloodred wine into a glass and hands it to Jack, heavily resting the bottle on the table. "Is good, I know this, but you taste, eh?"

"I believe you." Jack nudges the glass toward her with a broad smile stretched across his face, nodding at the bottle. "Are you the owner here?"

"Taste," the force of nature insists. She lets go of the bottle and crosses her arms under her ample bosom. There is no other way to describe the shelf of modestly constrained chest this woman has.

Jack lifts the glass and sips the dry red. "It's good, perfect," he says.

"Of course," she states on an authoritative nod, pouring a full glass for me before filling Jack's glass. "You listen to

Angelina; I no tell you wrong. Now"—she briefly assesses us—"Bolognese for you, and for the lady, my lasagna. You too skinny." And, with that, she marches toward the kitchen, barking in Italian.

I close my menu and pick up my glass of wine, taking a healthy sip. "I guess we're done ordering," I say, checking over my shoulder. The last thing I want is for Angelina to bust me making fun of her. "I wonder what we'll get for dessert."

"You think we'll get dessert?"

"If you clean your plate, you might. I'm too skinny, so I think I'm guaranteed to get mine."

"Oh, you're going to get yours; that's for damn sure." Jack's voice drops low, and he gives me a searing look that holds absolutely no mystery but all the promises in the world.

10

Jack

J ESUS *FUCK*, I DON'T know what I was thinking on the drive. *Why the hell did I get all personal?* That shit doesn't fly here any more than it does on a mission. Thankfully, Kate rolled with it and defused what was about to become a shitshow, all three rings running.

Angelina brings our calamari and an antipasto, telling us, "*Mangiate!*"

So, we eat and eat and eat as our newly adopted Italian aunt brings us more food than we can realistically manage.

"Oh my God," Kate sighs as she leans back from the table. "I'm so full." She spreads her hands across her flat belly, eyes wide and pleading.

We've hardly even touched our main courses, and I'm not going to lie, I'm kind of afraid of how little we've eaten.

"I'm not gonna make it through this," I say, scooping

another bite of pasta onto my fork. It's savory and thick, full of meat and covered in Parmesan cheese. The best I've ever had, including my time stationed in Italy. That was good, fantastic actually, but this tastes like *Zia* Angelina made it just for us. I pop the forkful into my mouth, effectively throwing Kate under the bus, since it would be bad manners to talk with my mouth full, and our plates are getting checked over.

Kate kicks at my shin, fully aware of my cowardice. "Angelina, this is amazing—"

"Of course it is." Nothing like the confidence in her craft this woman has.

"But I can't eat another bite. Can I take the rest with me? And maybe some tiramisu, too?" She smiles sweetly, and while I know it's not for me, that curve and pull of her lip and the pink blush of her cheeks burrow into my soul.

I push my pasta around my plate as I chew, afraid to put my fork down. Evidently, I can't win with this though because I get scolded for playing with my food. But small miracles, I also get my plate taken away with nothing more than a slap on the wrist.

"Jesus, she's scary as fuck," I murmur, leaning forward in my seat. No doubt, her hearing is as sharp as can be.

"Would you shut up? God help you, if I get guilted into putting one more thing into my mouth, I will literally die," Kate hisses, eyes wide. Her foot impacting with my shin again tells me loud and clear that she sees the lewd thoughts running through my head. "That includes your dick, so just don't right now. I swear, I'm going to explode."

"Let's go while we still can," I suggest.

Standing from the table, I get Kate's chair and help her into her coat, putting mine on as we step up to the hostess. I don't even bother looking at the bill, best to just pay it and cut sling load. I hand over my card and sign the slip as a huge to-go bag loaded down with food appears in front of me.

"Thank you, Angelina. Dinner was a memorable experience."

She hands me the bag, which is way too heavy to just be leftovers and dessert, and pulls me down to her squat level by the collar of my jacket. "You a good boy." She pinches my cheek, hard, and soothes it with a sound pat. "You take care of your girl. Make sure she eats enough, eh?" And, when she moves on to Kate, holding her at arm's length for just a moment, her eyes sparkle, and her lip mischievously curls up. "*Diventerai una brava madre,*" she says, soundly kissing Kate on each cheek.

My Italian is not great, but even I can figure out she's saying something about a good mother. I toss a couple of twenties on the signed bill and wrap my arm around Kate, leading her out into the cold evening.

"What did she say to me?" Kate asks as I hand her up into the truck.

"I couldn't tell you," I mumble, tucking the bag of food behind my seat and climbing in. I hit my GPS and wind out of town, toward the cabin I rented for the weekend.

While Kate spreads out on the couch, red-and-turquoise-striped socks kicked up on the coffee table, I fuck around with the fireplace until the cabin's living room is filled with the crackle and pop of the logs and the cozy glow of flames.

"That's quite the manly feat," Kate says as I plop myself down against the far arm of the leather sofa, tucking one foot under her ass for warmth and the other under her knees. Anything to be touching her. She pulls a blanket off the arm of the couch and throws it over her lap and my legs. "Tell me something." She soothingly runs her hand from my ankle to knee and back again.

"About what?" I scoot my ass down and lean my head back on the plush arm.

"Anything. Work. Home. Your greatest fears or what you want more than anything out of life." This is one of those soft moments where her accent hints at itself. Where there's more drawl to her words, melodic and relaxing.

"A lot of shit to cover there. We already touched on home, so work? I enjoy what I do. I feel a huge sense of purpose most of the time. The missions, the people, their faces, and gratification when we clear out the trash and make way for food and supply drops. No one likes a bully. Doesn't matter the color of your skin, religion, or even what grade you're in." I leave out the parts about hunting down the bully, infiltrating their strongholds, and taking them out in whatever way is necessary. Most people tend to like security better when they don't have to know the details of how it's attained and maintained. "What about you? Greatest fear?"

Kate snorts and shakes her head. "Born and raised in Miss'ssippi, but you know all that. I guess ..." She smooths the blanket, tucking it in around my legs. "Damn it. I guess my biggest fear is that I wasted way too much time on Chance, and I'll never ... eh, forget it. It's stupid."

I wiggle my foot, digging into her side with my toes, tickling. "Tell me."

She drops her head back, focusing on the dark wood beams stretched across the ceiling, her lips pursed with her thoughts. "I'm afraid I'll end up the spinster kindergarten teacher. That the only kids I'll ever have are the ones in my class." Her eyes close briefly before she rolls her head to the side to steal a glance at me.

My brows rise, and my mouth falls open in shock. "Are you kidding me? Because of that asshole? You sure as shit didn't turn the man gay, Kate."

"I know that. Deep down and rationally, I really do, but ..." She shrugs and shifts, turning so that her back is against the opposite arm of the couch and her arms are wrapped around her bent knees. All closed off, visibly protecting herself from the world.

And that's the last thing I want. It's one thing for me to lock up and compartmentalize, my job—my life at times—depends on that, but I want her to feel safe here with me. I'll have to examine the *why* of that later.

I reach under the blanket and pull her feet into my lap, wanting contact, needing to hold on, if just for now. "You're so much more than that. So much better than his shit." And it hits me, what Angelina said before we left the restaurant. "You'll have all of it, and you'll make an amazing mama someday."

She will. Jake has been talking her up nonstop since

school started. If I didn't know any better, I'd think that boy had been trying to set me and his teacher up. But that's ridiculous; he's five. A tiny dictator, entirely possible. But matchmaker? I doubt it.

"Mmm, maybe." Her jaw cracks with a wide yawn. "Not something to deal with today, but that's my fear. Total FOMO. What about you? Fears? Desires?"

I dig my thumbs into her arch, kneading the tension away. I don't want to tell her that I have the same fear. That I want the family life that Tripp has, but I'm scared shitless that I wouldn't be able to balance it with my job. That I'd fuck it up. And then it wouldn't just be my life I was ruining. That, if I had a family, people depending on me, and, God forbid, a mission went south, that would be the ultimate failure. One I'm not sure I'm willing to risk.

Instead, I slide my hands up her legs, wrapping my palms around the backs of her knees, and tug. Kate squeals as I pull her across the couch until her ass is nestled between my thighs.

"I'm afraid of falling asleep on this couch. And I desire nothing more than to lay you out across that big bed back there and worship every inch of your body."

Tossing the blanket aside, I scoop Kate into my arms, wrapping her legs around my hips, and stalk to the bedroom. And then I make my desires a reality. Peeling off her layers like I'm unwrapping my final Christmas present. The one you want to draw out and make last forever. I kiss, lick, and nip my way up her body, paying special attention to the dip of her hip, the sensitive skin under her tits. The hollow of her clavicle.

Pulling a sigh from Kate, I swallow a grunt and slide between her warm, creamy thighs, slowly fucking her. Drag and pull. Thrusting and grinding until I feel her clench and shudder, and only then do I let myself go.

11

Kate

I BARED MY SOUL, and now, it's just a matter of time until Jack pushes me away, and this thing ends. Dies an epic death. Our expiration date is looming, getting closer every single minute. But even I know that when a chick starts talking babies, guys typically run for the hills.

Though with the written-in-stone end date, it's been kind of liberating, knowing I can say just about anything because he's leaving regardless.

I slide from between the sheets and sift through the clothing strewed across the floor. The air is frigid, and the fire needs to be stoked. While I stir the embers and add another log from the basket on the hearth, I pray for some kind of coffee miracle in the kitchen.

As the steaming liquid gurgles out of the machine, hands slide around my waist, tugging me back into a hard wall of muscle.

"Morning," Jack mumbles into the rat's nest that is my hair. His nose brushes the shell of my ear as he pushes my hair to the side. Goose bumps run along every inch of my skin as he kisses down the column of my neck.

"Jack," I gasp as he pushes me into the edge of the counter.

His front is pressed to my back, contact from his lips down to our hips. The feeling that I handed this thing its deathblow by talking futures and babies dissipates in a puff of smoke and burning desire as Jack turns me and scoops me up onto the counter. All thought blows wide open as he pulls me to the edge and slides between my thighs, making me gasp and shudder. Carrying me while I'm still wrapped around him, Jack takes me to the bedroom where we lose ourselves in each other's bodies until we are nothing short of sated.

"You're going to have to feed me again," I say as I sit on the hearth to pull my boots on. "I'm weak."

Freshly showered, Jack appears at the edge of the room, jeans still unbuttoned, feet bare, T-shirt and flannel hanging from his hand. "We have a few leftovers," he teases. "We could just hole up here all day and—"

"Tempting but no. We need to go out in the world and see what there is to see."

He finishes dressing and shoves his feet into combat boots, pulling the laces tight and tucking the bows into the tops. "What?" he asks, straightening to his full height.

"Not a thing. Just surprised that I like watching you get dressed," I tell him, handing over his coat.

Jack huffs out a laugh and asks, "As much as you like watching me undress?"

"I'm usually too distracted to notice that." My smile pushes my cheeks high, and for the briefest moment, we stand there, staring at each other. Not with heated, lusty desire, but with something softer. Something scary and dangerous and … more. I clear my throat and grab my purse, murmuring, "Let's go." I duck out the door, needing to escape the fog of unattainable possibilities.

Sun bounces off the chrome grill of his truck, and the lights flash as the locks click open. Driving into town, down out of the mountain, is nothing short of gorgeous. Bright snow-covered trees line the road and guide us into the picturesque town nestled into the valley. I slide my sunglasses on and reach for the cupholder before I remember that it's empty, the cup I brewed in the cabin abandoned to lust. No coffee. None. And, if I don't fix that soon, I'm going to end up with a headache crippling me.

"A café sound good to you?" Jack asks.

"Dear God, yes. I need some caffeine and a big old plate of something bad for me," I groan. My stomach rumbles loudly at that moment, erasing any question on just how hungry I am.

Once again, defying logic and space constraints, Jack parallel parks his monstrosity and swings out to get my door. I like it. He's attentive but respectful. Masculine but not condescending. Long-term but leaving. I shove those thoughts and feelings away because I knew what this was, going into it. There's no use in dwelling on wanting to manipulate and change the outcome that is so solidly set in stone.

Instead, I focus on the late breakfast of eggs Benedict and breakfast potatoes with strong black coffee, trading bites for a taste of Jack's hash and egg skillet.

I grab the bill before Jack has a chance to set his coffee cup down and hand it and some cash to the server, telling her it's all good.

"Kate," he admonishes, reaching for his wallet. "Let me—"

"Nope. Breakfast is on me," I tell him, taken aback by the shocked look that crawls across his face.

"That's new." Jack stands, tucking his wallet away and reaching for my chair. He helps me into my coat, which, while a nice gesture, is usually more awkward than helpful. Reaching for and missing the sleeve, having to adjust and shimmy around until it's settled just right. But not with Jack. He manages to do even that with finesse and precision. "Thank you," he says, voice gravelly yet soft.

I turn to him as we step out onto the sidewalk. "It's breakfast. So not a big deal," I say, brows pulled together.

"Just has never happened to me before, a woman paying for a meal for me."

"Seriously?"

He shrugs, lifting one bulky shoulder. "Yeah, no. I'm not trying to be an ass, but I was raised to believe that the man pays. Opens the doors, all of that." He settles his hand at the base of my back and guides me down the street.

I let that idea simmer. Stir it around in my brain while we walk along the main street, peeking into shop windows.

"What are you doing for Christmas?" Jack asks as I peer into a stationery store, my love for books and journals pausing my feet.

"Going home to see my mama and them." He chuckles, and I realize that my Southern just flashed itself for all the world to see. "Sorry, my accent just does that when I think about going home."

"I like it." He nods to the door, asking, "Want to go in?"

I do, but the last thing I need is another journal, sitting empty on my shelf. Because let's face it; I love the beautiful books and all the potential their empty pages hold, but I don't want to mess them up with my ramblings.

"Nah, I need to find something for my mom and my friends. This would be purely a selfish store."

I'm a few steps toward the next little shop, the windows filled with handmade mugs and bowls, when Jack's palm lands on my back again.

"Do you mind if we go in here?" Mississippi has a serious thing for pottery, and my mother would love the gorgeous pieces and unique glazes.

"Not at all."

Jack gets the door once again, and as he strolls through the shop with me, I ask, "What about you?"

He pauses, brows lowered.

"Christmas. What are your plans?"

He picks up a small cream-and-brown mug, weighing it in his hands, almost like he's checking it for a good fit. "I fly home for a couple of days and then catch a flight overseas. Tripp'll meet me in Chicago, and we'll fly the rest of the way together." It feels like there's more he wants to say, like he's teetering on the edge of something, and instead of falling over, Jack takes an emotional step back. Forcing a smile, he replaces the mug and reaches for his phone. "Hey, I'm going to step out and take this. Are you good for a minute?"

"Of course. Take your time," I say.

He strolls out to the sidewalk and slides his phone to his ear. His broad back strains under the fabric of his coat, and he glances back at me before walking to the park bench a few stores down.

"Is there anything I can help you with?" a salesclerk asks. She straightens the mug Jack just walked away from.

Smiling, I say, "This is beautiful. Is it local?" I pick up a bowl glazed in blues and greens, the edge of it ruffled and a swirl of deep blue curling around the interior. It's just Lis's style.

"It is. In fact, the artist is due to stop in soon and drop a few pieces off." Her lips flatten into a tight line as she darts a quick look around the shop, nerves rolling off of her.

I tuck the bowl under my arm and move on to the next display.

"Oh, let me take that for you." The clerk scoops the bowl out from under my arm and protectively clutches it to her chest as she hurries to the counter.

A set of plates with soup bowls grab my attention, so I carefully add those to my bowl on the counter, almost dropping them as the shadow of a man appears in the doorway to the storage room.

His dark brown eyes skitter around the store, landing on where my hand curls around one of the soup-bowl-plate things. Silently, he approaches and places a crate on the floor behind the counter. "Nora," he says to the woman helping me, "these are ready to go. Anything you're low on?" He scratches at his chin, fingers getting lost in his beard, and scans the store, eyes landing back on my hands.

"No, I think we're good," Nora says quietly.

The interaction is kind of weird.

"There's a round platter in here that would go well with those soup-plates." He awkwardly nods at me. Shifting his weight, he steps back in the direction he came from.

"Okay." Nora watches as he disappears out the door as quietly as he came in.

"That was ..." I start, but I'm not sure where to take that statement.

"Intense. He's intense, very defensive of his craft." She relaxes visibly and asks, "Do you want to see that platter?" She sifts through the crate, pulling one beautiful piece of art after another out until she sighs. "Here we go," she says, placing a stunning platter in front of me.

Even though I'm sure it's way more than I'd normally spend, I can't walk away without it.

"My mama will absolutely love it. I think that'll be it though." I hand over my card and watch as she carefully wraps up my purchases, placing them in a beautiful red bag. Hell, with the bow she adds to the handle, I can use it as a gift bag for my mama's pieces.

I thank Nora and step out onto the sidewalk. Scanning the area, I find Jack leaning against the side of his truck, legs crossed at the ankle, hands shoved in his pockets and his eyes sparkling as he takes in my approach.

"You find something good?" Jack asks, reaching to relieve me of the bag.

"I did. Got my mama and one of my friends taken care of. I just need to find something for my roommate, and I'll be in good shape." I watch as he carefully sets the bag on the floorboard of the back seat of the truck. "How 'bout you? You get your call taken care of?"

"Yeah. Just confirming flight plans home for next week."

Next week. No matter how I cut it, I've not had enough time with Jack. I'm not ready for this to be done. I'm not ready to say good-bye. Instead of risking emotion spilling into my voice, I purse my lips and nod. I need to lock my emotions down. There's no use in showing my hand. Making things uncomfortable. It's not Jack's fault I'm falling for him, and it'll just be easier all around if I shove it down and ignore the way my heart beats faster, the way he's burrowed his way into my soul. He's leaving. It all comes back to the fact that he's leaving.

12

Jack

Each tick of the second hand is like a bomb timer counting down. Silent and ominous. Inescapable and unignorable.

The call I took gave me a headache and made me think about how much better Christmas would be with Tripp and his family or maybe in the Mississippi Delta as opposed to going home. Home. Home is so much more than a place on the map. An address. And the last place I want to spend the final days of my leave is with my judgmental family and the lying, cheating manipulator who tried her very best to fuck over my escape from them.

Jessica is ancient history. She just doesn't seem to be willing to acknowledge it yet. We dated through most of high school, and everyone in town had us practically married off at the start of my senior year. Yeah, no. By that point, I was pretty well on my way to the United States

Military Academy and wasn't going to do a damn thing to jeopardize that once-in-a-lifetime opportunity.

And, now, she's harassing me. Badgering me to get together while I'm home. Catch up. Over my dead body.

Of course, at the mention of our time coming to a close, Kate withdraws, turning inward. Shutting down. I close and lock the truck, her packages safely tucked over top of the bag from the stationer's shop. It didn't escape me, the way she stared at the gorgeous red leather-bound journal in the front window. I saw her hand drift toward where it lay in a bed of fake snow, bright mittens and a snarky coffee cup completing the display. I shouldn't have. It would be smart to let this thing with Kate die a natural death. Enjoy it until I left and then cut communication, go our separate ways. The thought of doing that physically hurts me; like a gut punch, it knocks the wind right out of me.

"You want to keep shopping or—"

"Yeah. I, uh"—Kate paints a tight smile across her face —"I need to find something for Gracyn."

I'm pretty sure that's her roommate, but since I haven't met any of these people, it's hard for me to be positive.

Words can't do a fucking thing to fix this, make it better, so I wrap my arm around Kate's shoulders. Pulling her into me, I plant a kiss at her temple and guide her down the sidewalk, seeking the next shop, the next little thing that will turn her smile from forced to full and real.

We wander in and out of stores as the sun dims behind clouds, the temperature drops, and the wind swirls snow flurries around us. I make damn sure to ignore my phone and the constant buzz of it in my pocket. I don't give a shit what Jessica is trying to orchestrate. I have Kate here within my reach, and that's all that matters. Live in the moment; tomorrow is never a guarantee—or something like that.

"That should do it," Kate says as a cashier hands back her card and gift bag stuffed full of tissue paper and what Kate claims is the perfect gift for her roommate.

Seemingly more relaxed than she was earlier, Kate tucks her wallet back in her tote, and I take the bag. As soon as I'm able, I wrap her other hand in mine and bring her knuckles up, pressing them to my lips. So soft. Her lotion hints at something clean and powdery. Something I can't quite pinpoint.

"What kind of lotion is this?" I breathe it in, committing the scent to memory, allowing it to seep into me so that I can carry it with me when I go.

"Mine?"

"Yes, Kate. Yours," I tell her.

She rolls her eyes, and as innocent or annoyed as that little movement is, all I can think of is how, when she comes, she does the same damn thing.

"It's called Au Lait. You like it?"

"I do." I inhale another hit of it, like it's a drug I can no longer live without.

Snow blows across the road as we climb back up the mountain to our cabin. Kate softly sings along with Sinatra, her voice sultry and deep, like she's a lounge singer from back in the day. Nothing is better than a whiskey-tainted voice—or, in Kate's case, tequila-tainted. Just one more damn thing about this woman that has me falling when I have no right to. No time for it. This isn't what I wanted. It's exactly what I was running from when I left Montana for West Point, New York.

I'm more than happy to play the bachelor uncle to Jake. I don't need anything more than that. The demands and expectations that my parents put on me to marry and stay on the ranch were fucking ridiculous. Sure, I'm their only son, but my older sisters married a few years prior, and their husbands liked ranching. Wanted to do it. I found my way out, and for some dumbass reason, I thought my family would be happy for me. Not what happened.

Instead of pride and congratulations, I got guilt and a fuck-ton of pressure to pass up the opportunity of a life-time. Honestly, earning an appointment to the military academy is one of the highest honors I can think of.

"What are you thinking on so hard over there?" Kate asks.

I didn't notice that she'd stopped singing with Frankie and Dean Martin.

"Nothing worth my time. You have fun today? Get everything set for Christmas?"

She hums her agreement as I pull into the drive for the cabin. The quiet shush of snow falling surrounds us. The flakes landing on Kate's bright red coat as we step out into the night is like a dusting of sugar. She looks good enough to eat.

I toss her a wolfish grin, trapping her in my arms as I reach around her to grab her shopping bags. "You want these inside, right?"

"I do." Kate reaches for the small bag partially hidden under the seat. "You want to take this in, too?"

I take it from her and tuck it back on the floorboard. "Nah, that can stay out. Nothing breakable in there." I don't know when I'll give it to her—hell, I'm not entirely positive that I will give it to her—but something about the way her eyes had lingered, like it was an extravagance, made me want to buy the thing.

"You found something for your mama then? For Christmas?" she asks, stomping the snow from her boots on the welcome mat.

I shift the bags to one hand and tap in the four-digit code, unlocking the door. "Meh, it's just a little something I didn't think I could pass up." I set the bags on the table and go straight to the fireplace, lighting the kindling, adding some logs. Coaxing some warmth into the room while steering her away from that line of questions.

The microwave dings, and Kate pulls out leftovers from last night, dividing the steaming pasta between a couple of bowls. "Is this good?" she asks, tucking forks and napkins into her hand and bringing it all to the rug in front of the fire.

"Perfect." I grab a bottle of wine from the grocery order I had delivered and pour us each a glass.

Kate twirls some pasta around her fork, shakes it off, and starts over again. "What's it like? Your job?" she clarifies when my brows pinch together, confused. "Can you even talk about it? Is that allowed?" She pops the pasta into her mouth, lips sliding the spaghetti from the fork.

"I can—"

"But you'd have to kill me," she teases.

"Yep. And that would be a waste." I swallow down some wine before continuing, "It's not very exciting until it is, and then time passes in perfectly choreographed chaos. Most of what I can talk about is the stuff you see on the news. Beyond that, I really can't." And I don't actually want to. I'll be back in the thick of it soon enough, and I took my leave stateside for an escape.

Kate nods, staring into the fire. "I don't know how Chloe and Jake do it. Do they get to talk to Dallas at all when he's deployed?" she asks quietly.

And this is why I can't do the family thing while I'm serving in this capacity. I know all too well how hard it is on the family left behind. "Not much. An occasional e-mail, maybe a call if the time zones and the mission starts line up just right, but when we're deep ..." I trail off, letting her make the natural conclusion.

"Wow. She's so strong, so stoic. Keeps Jake from losing his shit. She must not have the news on much around him, huh?"

"Probably not. Jake's a tough kid. This life is all he knows, so I think he pretty much rolls with it. Tripp has been popping in and leaving since he and Chloe got married. Hell, he missed most of Chloe's pregnancy. Almost missed Jake's birth, but that kid held out and waited for his dad to get home. He was a week late. Chloe said she was miserable, but I think, deep down, she was thrilled that Tripp was there for it."

We eat quietly for a bit, fork tines scraping against the plates.

"Y'all have been gone a lot then," Kate says, her accent coming out a bit.

"Mmhmm. But, when Jake was born, we were just out on an FTX—sorry, field training exercise—so it wasn't quite like it is now. Chloe called the CO's wife when she went into labor, and that woman was a teacup terrorist." I chuckle, thinking about how mighty my commanding officer's tiny wife was.

She sure as shit didn't let Army bureaucracy get in the way of what needed to be done. If she had an important message to get to her husband, she found a way.

"She made sure the colonel knew that Tripp needed to be fast-tracked home, and he fucking made it. There are some truly amazing people in the world."

Kate smirks over her wineglass. "Kind of makes up for the assholes causing trouble across the globe."

If only. I have seen some things. Things that sour my stomach and make my blood boil. Make me question whether God exists. I don't tell her any of that. What's the point? I deal with the bogeymen and the bad guys, so the rest of the world can rest easy.

13

Kate

WE SPENT TWO DAYS skiing in what I guess was a rare powder event in the Catskills and two nights wrapped up in each other. Drinking wine and eating dinner in front of a roaring fire. The only thing that could have possibly made the weekend better was a promise of a tomorrow. The possibility of a future even if that future was as simple as a date next week. A phone call next month. But, no, not here, not with us.

This weekend was good-bye. Tomorrow, I go back to work, and by the end of the week, we'll each be tucked in with our families, celebrating Christmas.

Not once have I had a desire to be anywhere but home for the holidays—until now. Snowy horse rides, crackling fires, wool socks, and mountains of blankets. That's how I picture Christmas in Montana. I'll be home in Hattiesburg, pretending it's downright chilly out and anything less than a puffy coat, scarf, and fingerless gloves is just asking for pneumonia. Meanwhile, I'll be tapping the AC a few degrees just so I can survive the heat. At some point over the past three years, I became a Northerner. Or at the very least, my blood's gotten thicker.

Jack's voice pulls me out of my thoughts as we approach Beekman Hills. "When do you head out? You are flying to Mississippi, not driving, right?" Taking his eyes from the road, he glances over at me.

"Flying, for sure. Wednesday afternoon. What about you?" I ask, wondering if we'll see each other even one more time before this is all over.

"Out of Newark on Wednesday morning."

"I'm out of LaGuardia."

The awkward tap dance, the back-and-forth of how to end things. Maybe it would be best to say good-bye today. A kiss at the door. *Thank you for a lovely weekend*, and leave it at that.

"I have a date tomorrow night with Jake, for dude time. It's tradition. But Tuesday? Can I see you then? Dinner maybe?" he asks, guiding his truck into a parking spot in front of my building, one that seems impossibly small.

I nod, biting at the inside corner of my lip. "Yeah, I can do that." The streetlights glow in the cold night, a haze illuminating out from antique-style fixtures.

"Good," Jack says quietly, stepping out of the truck.

Cold air invades the warm interior, and I pull my gloves on as he comes around to open my door. The manners on him. I'm sad. I hate that what we have is so short-term, but dear God, if I got nothing else out of the past month, I got my recalibration. I will not be wasting my time on any more trolls from this point on. My standards have been elevated.

Jack grabs my suitcase and a handful of shopping bags, leaving me with just my tote and a few smaller bags to carry. We climb the stairs in silence, and after unlocking my apartment door, I hold it open for him.

"Where do you want these?" he asks, slightly lifting my bags.

"Anywhere. By the hallway maybe? Can I get you a drink? Do you want to stay for a bit?" I need to get unpacked and ready for the last two days of school before Christmas break, but I don't want him to leave.

"Thanks, probably not though. I have some stuff to take care of"—he sets my things down—"and I would imagine you've got to get organized, too, yeah?"

He walks toward me until he's right there. A breath away. If I were to lean forward, I could bury my nose in the warm hollow of his neck.

Instead, I close my eyes and breathe in the scent that is all Jack—spicy citrus, a hint of leather. He slides his hands along my neck, thumbs lifting my chin so that my lips meet his. The kiss is soft, full of reverence. And over far too soon.

"Thank you for spending the weekend with me, Kate. I needed that more than you know." His lips brush against mine as he speaks. "I'll call and let you know what the plan is for dinner." Tilting my head, he presses his lips to my forehead; it's sweet, tender, so much more intimate than the chaste action should be. And he goes.

This is not good. Completely and totally bad actually. My heart is not going to come out unscathed; that's for damn sure.

I text Gracyn, wondering where the hell she is at ten on a Sunday night.

Gracyn: Working late. My boss is an ass.

Me: You work for your dad ...

Gracyn: Yep. Don't wait up. You have school in the morning. See you tomorrow maybe?

I send a kissy face emoji and pull my bottle of Casamigos Blanco from the cabinet above the fridge. Three fingers of oak-aged tequila will make doing laundry and organizing myself a little less painful. My playlists all feel just *too* much for my mood, so I browse through the categories, finally settling on something entirely *Jack*. Old-school Rat Pack. Crooners with voices rich and deep to balance the smoky caramel and vanilla notes of my drink and the melancholy that has descended on me.

I connect to my Bose speaker and let the music surround me, the tequila warming me, and I just start going through the motions of doing what needs to be done. I haven't been home much, not nearly as much as I normally am since hooking up with Jack. Gracyn, God love her, is not the neatest roommate in the world, but I guess the only other one I've spent a significant amount of time with was gay and ridiculously fastidious with his clothes and home decor. It's not a stereotype if it's true.

By the time I fall into bed, laundry done, apartment mostly cleaned, and supplies organized for two wild days in kindergarten, I think I should fall right to sleep. Sad to say, that's not how it works. Gracyn still isn't home, and I'm lonely. The apartment feels empty, my bed far too lonesome. I roll to my side and flop to my stomach, stretching out, reaching for the comfort of the person who's not there.

Two days of teaching kindergarten is a walk in the park. Unless it's the two days before the biggest holiday in these little kiddos' worlds. Add to that the disruption of having a substitute on Friday while I was off sexing it up in the mountains, and even the most seasoned teacher would be considering a career change right about now.

"Miss Beard, were you sick?"

"Miss Beard, that other lady didn't read the story right."

"Miss Beard, I missed you so much."

I knew I'd get a full rundown from these kiddos on the injustices of having a substitute change their routine.

What I didn't plan for was Jake.

"Miss Beard, Daddy said Uncle Jack went away with a pretty lady this weekend. Did you go away with Uncle Jack?" Jake pipes up just as I think the complaints, questions, and commentaries are winding down.

Laughing to try to cover the uncomfortable feeling of getting called out by a five-year-old, I ask, "Why would you think your daddy was talking about me?" *Sweet Jesus in a manger at Christmas.*

"'Cause, besides my mom, you're the prettiest lady I know," he responds, eyes wide and earnest.

"Aw, thank you, Jake. That was a really nice compliment. Hey, I have an idea." I sit down in my story-time chair. "Come sit on the floor for me, and how about we take a minute to go round the circle and give a little compliment to our friends?"

Nothing like thinking on my feet and finding a way not to lie to the little bugger. I know I can do it, but since we're pretty much guaranteed to not get a whole lot of book learning done today anyway, why not work on life skills? And saying something nice is never a bad idea.

Sitting and listening to these sweet children tell their friend to the left of them what they like, what makes them smile, what they're good at, it makes my heart happy. Some of the best teaching moments happen spontaneously, and all the planning in the world just can't compete.

The rest of the day and much of the next are spent on fun—giving crafts and activities for the kids with lots of time to share their thoughts and excitement for the coming break—and all the packing and organizing for me once school is out.

On Tuesday though, the last hour of school is dedicated to the winter party. Pin the Nose on the Snowman, Snowball Scoop with oven mitts and small white balloons. Sugar cookies and gifts galore. Books and coloring books for the kiddos. And so many thoughtful gift cards and coffee mugs and goodies for me.

And I finally get to meet Jake's dad.

"Miss Beard," Jake says in his playground voice, bouncing on his toes. He grabs my hand and wiggles it, trying to get my attention while I thank Cecelia's mom for all her help with the party. "Miss Beard—" Jake whines, all patience gone.

"Jacob Triplett, you simmer down and use your manners, sir," a deep voice commands.

Jake stops bouncing and shaking my hand but doesn't let go for a minute. "Yes, sir. Excuse me, Miss Beard, this is real important."

He turns his puppy-dog eyes to me, and I'm lost. An absolute goner. I squeeze his little hand and thank my party helper one more time before giving my full attention to Jake.

"Thank you for finding your manners, friend. What can I help you with?" I calmly ask him.

Jake smiles proudly and sweeps his free hand toward the giant of a man behind him. The one with the deep voice, soft eyes, and arm wrapped solidly around Chloe Triplett. "This is my dad. He and Uncle Jack are best friends, and they are soldiers and fight the bad guys."

I can totally see where Jake gets his sandy-brown curls.

Offering my hand, I say, "It's so nice to finally meet you, Mr. Triplett. Thank you for your service."

He takes my hand, firmly shaking it. "And thank you for yours," he says sincerely. "Jake talks about you all the time. All good things." He smiles broadly and winks at his boy.

"Ditto."

"Yeah, no need to sugarcoat anything. I'm sure he talks about Jack way more than me. Serious hero worship there."

"Maybe it's a phase?" I offer.

"It's all good. If I had to handpick someone for Jake to look up to, it would be Jack, all the way."

Jake beams up at his parents.

"Anyway, it was great to meet you. Enjoy your break. You've earned it with these heathens."

"Thanks so much, and y'all do the same. Merry Christmas."

I turn my attention to the class in general and get them ready to go. The class turtle is going home with Aubrey, the care instructions tucked into his food carrier. Flipping the chairs and shutting off the lights, I turn before locking my classroom door.

I couldn't be more ready for this little break, but I still have a few things to take care of once I get out of here. Most of my gifts were shipped home last week, but the ones I bought up in that little mountain town for my mama, I need to pad and pack, so they make it through the flight in one piece. And I want to make sure all of that is done and that my bags are ready to go before Jack picks me up in a couple of hours.

14

———

Jack

FINALLY, ON THE THIRD try, the lock clicks, and I push open the door to my room. Streetlight filters through the window, casting the room in a soft glow. It would be romantic as fuck if, for the life of me, I could think straight. But let's be honest; my blood has all gone south, and I can't process much more than getting to where I want to be. Where I need to be.

Kate drops her purse to the ground with a decided thud.

"You have enough shit in there?" I ask, chuckling.

She bites her lip and steps farther into the room, pulling at the belt tie on her ruby-red coat. Lord God, help a poor soldier. This woman is sexy as sin, even in the way she takes off her fucking coat. She might just be the death of me.

"Mmhmm, make fun all you want, but I do believe in

being prepared, and you know, if we need it, I probably have it in that bag," she states, dead fucking serious.

"I have everything we need right here." I toss my wallet to the table by the bed and slide the coat the rest of the way down her arms, dropping it to the floor.

And there she is. Standing in front of me in nothing fancier than jeans and a sweater, but damn the way her curves are hinted at beneath the bulky layers. I slide my hands along the sides of her neck, twining my fingers through her hair, and pull her in for a kiss. To savor or devour? Take my time and make this last, or rip her clothes off and ravage her until we're nothing but a sweaty mess in tangled sheets? This is it, and I'll be fucked if I'm not going to soak her in.

While my brain is trying to function on short rations, Kate's hands get busy, taking over. Working the buttons on my shirt, pulling it loose from my jeans. Shoving the material aside, she tickles and dances her fingertips down my torso, straight to my belt. She struggles with the buckle, getting nowhere fast, growling her frustration.

"You gonna laugh at me or help me with this?" she murmurs against my lips. "Why is this so hard?"

I try—really, I do—but I'm a guy, so pressing her hand over my hard dick, I snort out a laugh and tell her with all the honesty I possess, "You did that, sweetheart. That's all because of you." I shrug my shirt off the rest of the way and step into her. "Tit for tat, how 'bout you lose your sweater, so we keep things even?"

Before the words are fully out of my mouth, her sweater hits the growing pile of clothes on the floor. I flick open my belt buckle but catch her hands as they reach for me. I'm a grown-ass man, and I've got all kinds of control, but Kate makes me feel like a horny teenager, and one errant touch could have me coming in my jeans. And that's just not going to happen tonight. Hell no.

Holding her hands, I pull her toward me and kiss her again, parting her lips with my tongue, tasting her. Distracting her just enough to get myself back under control. Releasing her hands, I cup her tits, the lace straining over her tight nipples. The buds hardening against my thumbs while I hook my fingers into the cups, pushing the straps down off her shoulders. I kiss a trail from her lips, along her jaw and across her delicate collarbone. Dip my head and suck her nipple into my mouth, nipping at her through the lace.

Kate reaches behind herself, arching her back as she does, and pops the clasp, allowing her bra to drop away. Dear God, she takes my breath away. All that pale, creamy skin right there. Just for me. I guide her toward the bed and crawl up her body until she is splayed out, her chest to mine, touching everywhere we need to be touching.

Almost.

I push myself up and pop the button on her jeans, sliding them and her panties down those mile-long legs. I stand and grab hold of her boot-clad foot, unzipping one and then the other, peeling her jeans off and adding them to the mess.

"Katelyn, look at you. Fuck me," I mumble, working myself out of my briefs.

"That is the plan, right?" she asks, running her hands

up to her breasts, pushing them together, toying with her nipples.

"It is. You good with that plan?"

I pick up her foot, kiss the arch, her ankle, behind her knee, settling it on my shoulder. I repeat the sequence on the other side and slide down until I am face-to-pussy and give her a long, slow lick before circling her clit with my tongue. Kate's hips buck off the bed, a moan escaping from her lips as she grabs at my hair. I drag a finger through her slick heat and curl one and then two fingers into her pussy, pumping and sucking and flicking and stroking her to orgasm.

That's one, just to get her ready.

"Jack," she breathes my name on a shuddering sigh.

"You good?" I ask, reaching for one of the condoms in my wallet.

Kate hums her satisfaction as I rip open the black square and roll the condom down my length. I lean over, grasping my cock and rubbing it against her, slicking it up. Nudging her entrance, I push in partway and drop my forehead to hers. And that little hum that Kate had kicking a second ago turns to a moan as she adjusts. With small pulses, I thrust in deeper and deeper each time, gritting my teeth so that I don't fucking lose it. Her moan turns into a gasp as I push in that last bit until I'm fully seated, my balls tight up against her. Her eyes blown fucking wide.

"You still good?" I grit out—pausing not just for her, but for me, too, because my dick is being strangled right now. The life squeezed out of it in the best possible way. "Fuck, Kate. Tell me you're okay." I fight to keep my eyes open as her walls flutter around me. I want to know, see it in her eyes that she's ready to go.

"Gawd, yes. Oh my ... yes," she pants, rocking her hips. "Yes, Jack. *Oh-ma-Gawd*, yes." And she rolls back into me, stroking me. Fucking me.

And far be it from me to make this gorgeous woman do all the work. Retreating until just my tip is nestled in her tight heat, I thrust back in, moving her up the mattress. God, I could fuck her through time, forever. She makes me forget to breathe, forget my name. She almost makes me forget that I'm getting on a plane to hell in a few short hours.

She's the first woman who's made me want to miss a flight and stay right here, wrapped up in her.

But that can't happen.

"Jack?" she whispers, pulling me out of my head. "Are you ... what happened? Where'd you go?"

I shake all thoughts of leaving from my mind and focus on the woman who's breached my walls and crept inside my heart. "Right here. 'M right here," I tell her, punctuating each word with a kiss down her throat and a thrust of my hips. Each thrust ending with an extra push to get closer, deeper, etching the feel of her permanently on my soul.

Her nails dig deep, piercing the skin on my back, marking my ass as she pulls me tighter still.

"Jack ..." she gasps.

I curl down on the next thrust and take her nipple into my mouth, sucking hard, cutting off her words. Biting just the way she likes, and she comes. Hard. Body shaking, muscles pulsing, head thrown back, arching into me. Eyes rolling back, lashes fluttering against her pink cheeks. I thrust two, three, four times, wanting to wring out every ounce of her pleasure before I explode.

And I do. A blinding fire races up my spine, and all I can think of is Kate. Beneath me, around me, consuming me.

"Jesus, how did you do it?" I ask before my brain completely comes back online. I push myself up, trying not to crush her, but she firmly holds me in place. "I don't want to crush you."

"You're not. I love feeling your weight on me. So solid, so ... you make me feel safe, secure." She runs her fingers through the hair at the back of my head. "How did I do what?"

"Huh?"

"You asked how I did it ... what did I do?" she hums, wrapping her legs around mine, hooking her feet under my calves.

Fuck. I'm pretty fucking sure I can't tell Kate I'm falling for her. Not now. Not when I'm leaving in a matter of hours, and I have never dropped into a mission with a girl-friend back home, counting on me to make it out alive. There are too damn many unknowns. All the messy complications that I've worked so hard to avoid.

"Swear I blacked out for a minute." I slide out of bed and take care of the condom before curling myself around Kate's relaxed, sated body.

And, as I drift off to sleep, I hear her whisper, "Thank you" and feel the press of her lips to the palm of my hand.

After a few hours of the best sleep I think I've ever had, I shower and throw on my clothes. I dropped my truck off at Tripp and Chloe's yesterday afternoon, swapping it for a rental to get to the airport. I'm fucking hard-pressed to find any desire to walk out of here though.

Light from the partially opened bathroom door slants across the room, highlighting Kate's sleeping form. Her creamy skin glows in the soft light, calling to me, begging to be tasted and caressed one last time.

If I wake her to say good-bye, it'll just be hard on her. On me. So, I do what any cowardly piece of shit would do. I sweep her hair aside and kiss the back of her neck, lingering for an extra beat. Inhaling the scent of her skin, committing it to memory before stealing away.

Her overstuffed tote bag is still where she dropped it after dinner last night, the top gaping open. I pull the wrapped journal from my ruck and tuck it into her bag. Fuck knows when she'll actually find it with all the shit she carries around in the name of preparedness. Hopefully, she takes the granny shears out before she tries to go through TSA.

My eyes dart over to her one last time as I reluctantly ease out the door.

15

Kate

MY PLANE TOUCHES DOWN in Hattiesburg, and the minute we get the go-ahead from the flight crew, I turn my phone back on. Desperate for a text from Jack and hating myself for it. The only new texts I have are from Gracyn, gushing about the Christmas present that I left on her bed and bitching about her asshole client. Her daddy runs the family accounting firm and seems to think he's got the right to handpick a douche-bag husband for her. According to Gracyn, he's nothing but a highbrow asshat, cheating on her mama and alienating his kids at every turn.

My mama and daddy, on the other hand, couldn't be any sweeter on each other.

I shuffle off the plane, stopping in the restroom on the way to baggage claim. The slash of red marring my panties has never been more welcome after the unfortunate condom debacle. Along with a deep sigh of relief and tension flooding from low in my belly, it's entirely possible that I do a little happy dance in my stall after putting myself back together.

On the short walk to grab my checked bag, I send a quick note to Jack.

Me: Have a fantastic visit home. Also … got the all-clear from Aunt Flo. No mishap from the ill-fitting oops!

I drop my phone in my tote, next to the pretty wrapped present that magically appeared in there overnight. Part of me wanted to open it the minute I saw it, but mostly, I wanted to wait. For what, I don't know, but it's still wrapped, still in my bag. Still a symbol of mysterious possibilities.

Naturally, my suitcase is just about the last one off the plane, but the minute I have it, I pull my phone back out and call my daddy, letting him know I'm ready. As I end the call, I check my messages and see dots bouncing from Jack. They start and stop several times, finally ghosting and disappearing entirely.

I shove down my disappointment and roll my bag to the curb where my daddy pulls his shiny red truck to a stop in the middle of God and everybody.

"Hey, sunshine," he calls, hopping out, rounding the front side and giving me a big bear hug. "Good to see you again." He holds me at arm's length, smile stretching his mouth wide.

"Hey, Daddy." I plant a quick kiss on his cheek and look to the line of cars stacking up behind where he stopped, essentially blocking traffic. Bless his heart.

Airport security is for everyone but him. "Think we should load these up and head on out?" I collapse the handle of my big rolling suitcase.

He looks to the left, taking in the annoyed faces peering at us through windshields. Smirking, he nods, and then grabs my bags and setting them in the back seat.

Yep, my daddy, Dennison Beard, with his brown hair streaked with bits of silver and tortoise-shell glasses drives a big ole truck. The man is president of a bank. A pretty sedan or lush SUV would fit him so much better, but he's a Southern boy through and through. Pickup truck and business suit.

We climb in and head into town, passing familiar landmarks.

"Gonna have to drop you home and head on back to work for an hour or so. Your mama's in there, baking, I think." He spins the steering wheel, bouncing us up the drive, stopping next to the house I grew up in. "You go give your mama some love, and I'll carry your bags up to your room and see y'all for supper." He gets my door and pulls my bag from the back seat in quick succession. Then, he bounds into the house.

This is the man who set my expectations so high. How did I fall so far? Being with Jack for the past month has reminded me of my worth. That it's good to have high standards because, if I don't have them for myself, no one else is going to have them for me.

"There she is," Mama says brightly as I push through the kitchen door.

"Hey, Mama." I wrap my arms around her, feeling like I

just stepped back in time. This house, this kitchen, the smells—it all brings me back to the very best childhood I could've asked for.

"My God, I have missed you," she drawls, squeezing me extra tight. "When are you coming back home? There's plenty of teaching jobs here, you know."

I do know. Maggie Hays Beard reminds me of that fact every time we talk.

"Maybe you and Daddy should come visit me in New York. Y'all just might like it."

The front door bangs shut, and my father's truck roars to life, the rumble fading as he takes off down the street. It doesn't escape my notice that my invite to visit has gone unacknowledged. Sometimes, I think my parents purposely stay away from New York, avoid visiting me because they might just like it up there the same way that I do. They've wanted me to come back home since Chance and I broke up. They still don't know the reason behind that shitshow, and if they acknowledge how beautiful it is up north, they might just have to give up their campaign for my return.

"Well, let's get to it, baby. We've got cookies to make and pies to bake," Mama says instead. "Tell me about those little darlings you have this year. Who had to take the damn turtle home this break?" She rummages around the cabinet under the island, pulling bowls and cookie sheets out for a full evening of baking.

"It's a coveted honor to take Dash home." Yeah, I didn't name the turtle Dash for his dashing looks. He actually moves pretty quickly for a turtle. Early on, when I was cleaning his cage, I about lost him as he scurried across the floor, heading straight for the kindergarten commons. "And it's a highly selective process. Grades, good behavior—"

"Willing parents," she finishes for me.

And I just laugh because it's absolutely true. So many families travel over the break, so it's sometimes hard to find anyone willing to pull turtle duty.

"Who's your favorite this year? Still that one little boy, Jackson?"

My heart stutters at her mistake. "Jake, yeah. His daddy came home for leave. I don't know how he and his mom do it, being apart all the time, but Jake was so happy and proud when he introduced us yesterday. He was absolutely beaming."

"Bless them." There's more than one meaning to that phrase in the South, but this time, Mama is full of sincerity.

My family holds service to the country in the highest regard. My great-grandpa served during World War II, and the stories I've heard about what he saw would send chills down your spine and turn your hair white.

The rest of the evening passes in a whirl of food, conversation, and catching up. My brother, Sam, even stops by for a hot minute with my three-year-old niece, Harper, in tow.

"Y'all leave your mama home alone, Harp?" I ask, tugging on one of her curly brown pigtails.

Harper wiggles in my arms, trying to get to the rack of cookies cooling on the counter.

"Yeah, Jules isn't feeling so great right now," Sam says, snagging a cookie and breaking it in half. He blows on one piece before handing it to his daughter.

"Uh-oh. She caught a bug or somethin'? You tell her not to worry about bringing a thing to Christmas dinner. Kate can help me with everything." My mother pours some milk into a sippy cup, handing it to Harper. "Here ya go, darlin'."

Sam mumbles, "Something," and snags a couple of more cookies, smirking at me from across the kitchen.

I open my mouth, but he shakes his head and cuts his eyes to Super-Mimi, his nickname for our mother when she's in full grandma mode. Looks like we're going to have another baby to spoil next Christmas.

"All righty, Harper, let's hit it. Auntie Kate needs her beauty sleep, so she can hang with us cool kids." He quickly hugs me, whispering his plea to keep the surprise under wraps.

He plucks Harper from my arms and tosses her in the air. Harper squeals with delight, and Mama admonishes Sam with a smack of a kitchen towel even though he never actually breaks contact with his precious baby girl.

SLOWLY BLINKING AWAKE, I roll over and swipe my phone off the nightstand. Still nothing from Jack. Not a word. I guess he wasn't as concerned about our blowout as I thought he was.

Tossing my phone aside, I take a quick shower and throw on jeans and a super-lightweight sweater. It's significantly warmer than I'm used to, but if I go out in just a T-shirt, the winter-minded people of Mississippi might just shiver in their UGGs. And that just won't do.

"Morning, baby," Mama greets, handing me a cup of coffee in a hand-thrown mug. She does love her pottery. "After you eat, I'm gonna need you to run out to the grocery store for me." She fills a plate, setting it on the island in front of me with a napkin and fork.

"Jesus, are you trying to fatten me up?" I ask, looking at the homemade biscuits swimming in a pool of creamy gravy.

As a silent response, she plops a heaping spoonful of sausage crumbles on top and starts writing up her shopping list.

"Sam's dropping Harper by on his way to work. I hope whatever Jules has isn't contagious," Mama muses.

I hide my chuckle behind my napkin. God, she's going to lose her shit when Sam and Jules tell her they're expecting again.

Any complaints I had about my huge breakfast are nothing but lies. My plate all but licked clean, I shove my feet into my Chucks and grab my purse, Mama's list, and the keys to her Lexus. "Call me if you think of anything else while I'm out," I toss over my shoulder.

I check my phone before pulling out onto the street. I check it again when I park at the store. I hate that I'm checking it again as I push my buggy past the refrigerated cases to the whipping cream. Disappointment settles in my heart at the lack of any new messages.

"Well, hey there, Katie. You lookin' for a text from me?"

There's only one person that voice could possibly belong to, and I'll be fucked if it's the last person I feel like dealing with.

I place my carton of cream in the buggy and straighten, pasting a fake-as-shit smile on my face. "Chance, hey." I skate my eyes over his shoulder, scanning the area. "You finally bring your boyfriend home to meet the family?" I ask.

He stiffens and swings his head around, checking to see if anyone overheard me. "Would you hush?"

Oh Jesus.

"You still haven't told them? Bless your heart," I say, pushing down the aisle to the cheese case. And, yeah, this is the other kind of *bless your heart*—the *fuck you* version.

Chance wraps his hand around my arm, halting me. "I haven't," he whispers. "You know how my daddy is. He'd just die. And that would break my mama's heart, and you know it."

It's true. All of it, but I just can't really find it in me to care. I peel his hand from my bicep and cross my arms over my chest. I owe him nothing. Not a damn thing, but he's shifting on his feet and bouncing his hip, his tells for having some favor to ask. How did I not notice in all the years we dated that Chance acted like one of my girlfriends? Am I just now noticing this after all the time I spent with Jack over the past month?

"So, do you want to hang out while you're home? Maybe come by for dessert after y'all have Christmas dinner tomorrow?"

Blink. Blink. Blink. "Are you—"

"Kate, help me. Just this once. I swear, I'm going to tell them soon. Just ... just help me get through the holidays, and then I swear to God, I'll come out," he pleads.

Really? Really?

"Go to Hell, Chance." I shake my head in disgust and walk away.

"Kate?" he calls, still not seeing how fucked up what he's asking me to do is.

Hastily, I grab the last few things I need from my list and wave over my shoulder. "Say hey to your mama and them. Merry Christmas, Chance." I pay and haul ass to the car, cranking the AC once I'm settled in the driver's seat. And, because I really am a desperate fool, I check my phone one last time—I promise.

Jack: Check. Merry Christmas. Thanks for everything.

Thanks for everything? That nothing of a response takes the wind right out of my sails. Right or wrong, I wanted more. I could call him. Fake that I never received his text and tell him again that we're in the clear, but suddenly, all I want to do is go home and take a nap. I'm tired. I'm sad.

I just want to crawl into my bed and nurse my serious case of the blues.

16

Jack

"YOU'RE HOME."

That voice, almost as much as the question itself, causes tension to coil under my skin. This is one of the many reasons I don't like coming back home. So many damn people tried to keep me here, thinking they had my best interests at heart. In fact, they all had their own agenda at the forefront of their minds.

I turn to face my ex-girlfriend and take a step back when I see she's not alone. "Jess." It's curt, maybe too curt, but I sure as fuck am not thrilled to see her. I just want to grab the handful of things my sister asked me to pick up in town and get my ass out to the ranch. Face the next round of interactions that will confirm the wisdom of my decision to leave Montana and choose a completely different life. My skin feels too tight here, constricted.

Jess takes half a step toward me, a tentative smile painted across her face. "It's so good to see you again, Wyatt."

I bristle at the use of my first name. It's something I primarily associate with negativity. With home. With the need to run.

"You look good. Really good," she continues, her hand fluttering from the shoulder of the young girl standing with her to the base of her throat. A simple gold band on her left ring finger.

There is so much wrong with this picture. So fucking much, and I'm not sure if I don't know what to say or if I just don't care to say anything at all.

Jess stills, following the line of my gaze, and makes a fist, shoving her wedding-banded hand into the pocket of her parka.

Shaking my head, I step to the side, essentially putting her daughter between us before replying, "Nice to see you, too, Jess."

And the poor kid, twelve years old now—or she will be soon at least—has her head on a swivel, looking from her mother to me, probably wondering what the fuck is happening.

You and me both, kid.

I offer my hand, introducing myself, "I'm Jack. Went to school with your mom a million years ago."

"Charlie." The girl shakes my hand and screws up her face. "Jack or Wyatt? Which is it?" Charlie looks at me with all the attitude of a self-centered kid with nothing more than popularity on her mind.

The apple doesn't fall far from the tree.

"Wyatt Jackson. My friends call me Jack," I tell her.

"So, why'd my mom call you Wyatt?"

Why fucking indeed? Because she's a backstabbing, manipulative liar.

Obviously, that story isn't one that gets shared on the regular, but I don't need to be an asshole. Not at this given moment anyway and sure as shit not to a kid.

"Ancient history. You have a merry Christmas." I nod and walk purposefully away, gathering the list of shit Dana requested.

I didn't even make it out to the ranch before my past started rearing its ugly head. File this under reasons I don't come home.

Thank God I stopped for a bottle of tequila before leaving Missoula. I'm gonna fucking need all the help I can get to make it through this visit if this is how it's getting started.

I make it through the aisles, manage to pay, and escape to the parking lot, plastic grocery bags hanging from my left hand. Relief is sweet but fleeting as I pop the trunk of my rental car, and Jess sidles up, leaning against the truck in the next spot over. She stares as I place the bags next to my duffel.

"What is it, Jess?" I ask, patience gone.

"I want to see you while you're home. Spend some time with you, reconnect."

I glance around the lot, her daughter nowhere in sight.

"Yeah? Not gonna happen," I tell her, slamming the trunk closed. "I told you last week, I'm not interested. And

I'm pretty sure your husband wouldn't be all that thrilled at the idea."

She's blocking my access to the driver's side of the car, arms crossed, looking a little more brazen with Charlie out of the direct line of fire. "I've never loved him, Wyatt. You were the one I wanted."

A huff pushes out of my nose. "Got a fucked-up way of showing it. You get Charlie's father to marry you? Or did you trick some other poor bastard into thinking he knocked you up?"

"I married her father right after graduation but only because—"

"Because your father found out who was really responsible," I finish, cutting off whatever bullshit excuse she was about to spew at me.

"I didn't have any other choice," she yells, her arms swinging out before they slap down at her sides.

"In what? Getting pregnant or trying to pin it on me?" Disgust drips off of my words. "Doesn't fucking matter, honestly. You knew I didn't want this life, that all I wanted was to get out of here, and you tried to sabotage the only way it could happen. I didn't want anything to do with having a family, Jess. And you tried to rip all of that out from under me."

I don't know how many times we've had this argument in the past decade, but I'm over it. So fucking over it.

"And now?" she asks, sniffling. It could be the cold, but everything about this whole interaction screams devious posturing.

"Nothing's changed, Jess. I'm happy with my life and not moving back here, so it doesn't matter." Manipulation or not, I soften my features, relaxing my stance. Mixing things up, putting Jess at ease, might be just enough to throw her off her game. Switch up the balance of power.

Jess visibly relaxes, moving with me as I saunter around the side of the car. With each of my steps forward, she takes one back until she's far enough past the door that, when I click the lock button and pull at the handle, the door is a physical barrier between us.

"Go home to your husband, Jess. Raise your daughter with a good sense of right and wrong. Google that shit if you need to. But you and me? We're done. Don't contact me again. I'm not fucking interested." I close the car door, her face a mask of shock at my dismissal. I think I was really damn clear, leaving no room for doubt.

And, as I drive out of the parking lot, a middle finger in the air and Jessica's back are all the confirmation I need that this mess is finally done.

I feel for the kid. Hope she gets a fighting chance because her mother is batshit fucking crazy.

SNOW-COVERED FIELDS WITH PRAIRIE grass peeking through the crust line my drive out to the ranch, giving me a chance to refocus and prep for the next round of guilt and pressure to move back home. But not even that serenity is enough to temper the passive-aggressive bullshit that's thrown at me the minute I walk through the door.

"You ready to do some real work for a change, boy? Got fences need fixed and ..." my father bellows as soon as I breach the doorway.

The only reason he's here at the house at this time of day is to give me shit and lay me low for walking away. For the love of fucks, you'd think I left to go pursue fashion design in the big city. And that thought does nothing but land Kate front and center in my mind.

I set the grocery bags down on the kitchen table, gritting my teeth to hold back a smart-ass comment that will get me nowhere. I've fought with enough crazy today; it's safer in the desert.

"Thanks," my sister Sophie says, looking way too tired to be bustling around the kitchen. "Heard you ran into Jess at the store. How'd that go?" She unloads the bags, sorting items Dana asked for as she does.

"You coming, Wyatt? Time you pitch in around here for a change," Wyatt Senior throws at me.

Yeah, there's not a damn thing wrong with the name Wyatt. I just hate the bastard I share it with.

Sophie looks up at me and shrugs before going back to her task. I don't know why I expected any help from her. My entire family is on board with wanting me to come home. More hands make for lighter work.

"Give me a minute to change," I huff out.

The fight is not worth it.

I grab my duffel and take it up to my old room. Not a damn thing has changed there in all the time I've been away. Well, almost nothing. Every single thing that came home from West Point with me is gone. My annuals, pictures, my cadet uniforms, and even my saber—all gone. The life I wanted, the things I accomplished with blood, sweat, tears, and determination have so little meaning to those who can't see beyond their own front door. I pray that I can find my things later—when I have time to sift through the closet, through boxes in the attic. For now, I bite my tongue, change into jeans, and shove my feet into my old work boots, noting that they're still here. The worn leather cleaned and conditioned. Because ranch work has value. Being a soldier, not so much.

My old man is outside in the warm cab of his truck, smoking and glaring. Not at anything in particular. It's just his version of resting bitch face. Reluctantly, I climb in next to him. We ride in silence out to a remote line of fence that's needed to be fixed for years, my brothers-in-law nowhere in sight.

Throwing the truck into park and cutting the engine, my father barely glances my way. "Gloves and work coat're in the back," he grunts before he swings himself out and starts pulling supplies from the bed.

I lock down my anger and grab my work gloves and beanie, swapping out my jacket only because the one I brought really isn't for ranch work. But who the hell thought I'd be running fence wire before even saying hello and merry Christmas to my mother? If this is the game my old man wants to play, I'll fucking win.

Trudging through the snow, I get as far away from him as I can manage. Jaw clenched, not a single motherfucking curse passes my lips as I set to work, my mind churning over the shit day this has already been.

I work for hours, silently pulling and securing wire, ignoring the big fucking elephant that has parked his ass on the prairie between us. I've got nothing to say to the bastard. Not a goddamn word.

As the light fades, my phone pings, pulling me from my almost-meditative state. I drop my gloves and swipe the screen to see a message from Kate.

Kate: Have a fantastic visit home. Also ... got the all-clear from Aunt Flo. No mishap from the ill-fitting oops!

Thank Christ she's not pregnant. I'm not sure what I would have done with that. I tap out a quick reply and shove my phone back into my pocket because I swear on all that is good and holy, I will finish this job. Get well beyond the meet-in-the-middle point and show the old bastard that I can not only just hold my own, but I can also kick his ass while doing it. Fuck him and his claims of old-man strength.

The sky darkens as I fix the last of the wire and load the remaining supplies and tools in the back of the farm truck. I climb into the warm cab, debating on the benefits of riding back to the house, cradled in warmth but subjected to more stony silence, or freezing my ass off in the bed with the tools, blanketed under the stars twinkling in the clear sky. I don't hate Montana. I just never wanted to be forced into staying here.

When I'm back at the house, the night passes in a flurry of passive-aggressive bullshit, though the meal is good, evoking some of the few good memories of living here. Farm work makes a man a different kind of tired, and though I've humped my ass in and out of some hairy shit overseas, I fall into bed, exhausted.

It's not until well into the next morning that I realize that I forgot to hit Send. And, the minute I do, all hell breaks loose, and any thoughts of texting Kate fly out the window.

17

Kate

A CASE OF THE blues, my ass.

Gracyn might have the blues, pining after the one who got away. But I'm thinking I could be coming down with something. You know that feeling when you're on the edge of having a stomach bug, and you just want it to kick in, so you eat like shit in hopes of getting it started, so you can just get over it? Yeah, I'm there.

Absences from school are always up this time of year, but we seem to be on the front edge of a stomach virus, and I am exhausted from sanitizing all the surfaces in my classroom. Add to that my genius idea of having a student of the week. Not a bad thing in and of itself, but this week's student was so excited that he didn't want to miss anything, so he didn't run to the restroom before reading time, and he peed all over the upholstered bench I'd brought into school this semester.

Needless to say, story time was cut short, and I need a damn beverage. I pull my phone from my desk drawer and about have my SOS text fully typed when one comes through from Gracyn, thinking she's had a week already. Bless her heart—and that one is totally of the bullshit variety. It's only Monday. I feel like I haven't seen my girls in forever, and let's face it; I really need that drink, so I hit her back, telling her I'm in, and thankfully, Lis can make it, too.

Lis is already set up at the bar when I walk into McBride's at four thirty. Her auburn hair twisted up in a messy bun, a pint of beer in her hand.

"Hey, sugar," I say, leaning in to give her a hug.

Finn reaches for my bottle of Patrón, but I wave him off.

"I think I'll just stick with beer today. Thank you though."

"Where've you been? I feel like I haven't seen you in forever," Lis says.

And it has been a while. I take a big pull of my pint and press my palm to my chest.

"You okay?"

I squinch up my mouth like I just sucked on a lemon and respond, "Yeah, mostly. Just a little icky in my tummy."

It'd be just my luck to get the stomach bug that runs through the elementary school about this time every damn year.

The door to the pub opens, letting in a blast of cold air. Finn tosses a coaster on the bar beside me and has a full pint ready to go by the time Gracyn dumps her jacket on the back of the barstool. And, even though she drains half of the glass in one shot, she declares that it's a whiskey night for her. We chat for a hot minute, laying out all the badness of the Monday-est of all Mondays. Lis, a nurse, got puked on by a patient; I share the love of my story-time adventures; and Gracyn mumbles about her bad week.

Then, Gracyn turns to me, saying, "How's it going with your mystery man? I feel like I haven't seen you since that night you were on your way out to meet him."

It's true; we have been kind of missing each other. A wave of longing washes over me, and I know that, if I don't lighten the mood, I might just let a tear escape. And that would be a whole lot more talking than I feel like doing just now. So, I go for funny and lewd because that's certain to keep the deeper questions at bay. I'm just not ready to go there yet. "Mmm … he's good. Really fucking good." I let my accent out to play, and the words come out, all kinds of Southern-fried.

"Yeah?" Gracyn asks. Her side-eye game is strong tonight. She has a tendency to do that when she's avoiding her own mess. "Is he the one to break your bad luck?"

Has he ever. My stomach lurches when she asks if they'll get to meet him soon. Every cell in my body is yearning for him again, to feel his touch, to have him near. To know that he's safe.

I call to Finn and order a platter of whatever they have that's deep fried.

"Not gonna happen, darlin'," I tell her. "He's gone already. He, um … he was here, visitin' between deploy-ments. Took off back to one of the 'Stans—Kyrgyzstan,

Kazakhstan—something like that. But it was lovely while it lasted."

Both Lis and Gracyn stare at me, dumbfounded, glasses paused midair.

Gracyn sets hers back on the bar and asks, "How did this happen? Where did you even meet him?"

"Y'all know how you were asking me about parent conferences? And if I met any hot, divorced dads?" I launch into talking about Jake and his enthusiasm for his uncle, and though I try to hide it, it's obvious they both know that Jake's my favorite student. I would make him student of the week every week if I thought I could get away with it.

Lis smiles at me, and Gracyn shakes her head as I talk.

"Uncle Jack came and had lunch with Jake, and, Gawd, the way he squished that big ole body of his into the kindergarten lunch table ... y'all just don't even know."

Thankfully, Finn interrupts, setting the food in front of us. "Gracyn, give us the deets on the shite at your office. I couldn't believe I missed the lead-up," he says, surveying the bar area for glasses in need of refilling.

I dig into the deep-fried carbs, dragging a chicken finger through the various dips before popping it into my mouth. According to Finn and Gracyn, there was a knock-down, drag-out fight at the accounting firm that Gracyn's dad owns.

Lis and Gracyn nibble on the platter of snacks, but it seems as though I'm the only one really putting the food down. And, thankfully, that's not too unusual for me.

Finn nods to a customer and pulls a fresh pint for him.

When he settles back in front of us, he crosses his arms over his chest and jumps back into his story about the fight. "The bougie little prat started the whole thing," he says, absolutely incensed.

While I'm only half-listening, my stomach rolls again, and I have to concentrate on making sure it stays put. For a girl who can put away some serious alcohol, I am not a good puker. If I'm going to get sick, the last place I want it to happen is here at the pub. No, I'd much rather be home, in my clean bathroom where no one can hear me.

I'm considering leaving, just in case, when Gracyn swallows hard and grips the edge of the bar.

"You're sure?" she asks. "It was Gavin Keller? *The* Gavin Keller?"

Color drains from Gracyn's face, and I meet Lis's eye. I might be the queen of dating disasters, but Gracyn's been messing around for almost two years, trying to fight what's turned out to be true love with this guy. She's been busting her ass at work to get a couple of days off, so she can go see him in LA before his band, The UnBroken, leaves on their European tour. They've spent so little time actually with each other, and now, with his tour starting, it's going to be even more of a struggle.

I pull my phone out at the same time as Lis and type Gavin's name into the search bar, perusing the headlines.

"Holy shit, he missed the first show. *Tour musician stands in for Keller. Will this be a permanent change?*" I scan down the seemingly endless hits on Google, stopping on a blurb from gossip site, theBuzz. "Oh my Lawd, listen. *Gavin Keller was arrested and detained stateside on assault charges. Speculation is that Keller is taking after bandmate Kane Newton and tapping that which can be tapped.*" I look up at Gracyn's stricken face. "Sorry, probably should have stopped before I hit that last part." I shrug, but I have a feeling this is bad.

Gracyn stutters, starting and stopping a million questions to no one in particular. She pauses and almost looks like she might pass out for a minute. Out of nowhere, she screeches, "That fucking bastard! He knew. He sat at that dinner, knowing full well how pissed I would be."

The grease-laden food suddenly too much for me, I lean back from the bar while Gracyn calls her slimy client every name in the book.

"I'm gonna have to tell my dad, and—"

Finn cuts her off, looking uncomfortable, "Gracyn, love, your da was there. He called the cops."

Lis flashes us a picture on Instagram from the client dinner Gracyn attended on Friday. It's bad. To anyone who hasn't been around Gracyn and heard the stories of this client, the fucking bastard, it looks like nothing short of an engagement photo. Her hand on his chest, face tilted to his smiling one, the two of them surrounded by their parents.

"Well, shit. That sure looks bad," I say.

I should have bitten my tongue instead because Gracyn drops her tumbler, glass shattering across the floor. Shards jump up and bite at my ankles, skittering off the leather of my boots.

Lis jumps from her seat as Gracyn sways on wobbly legs. I reach for her arm, wanting to steady her, offer support of some kind, but Gracyn braces her hands on the edge of the bar and shakes her head.

"Gracyn? Are you okay?" Lis asks.

I mean, we all *know* she's not okay. Who would be if your father had the man you loved thrown in jail for not being the one he'd chosen for you?

But my roommate doesn't say a word. She just stands there, knuckles turning white as she grips the scarred, lacquered oak. It takes Finn and a broom to finally drive her away from the spot she's anchored to.

I slide out of my seat and shrug on my coat, leaving the belt untied. The greasy food might have seriously done its thing because my stomach is rocking and rolling. But Gracyn needs me, so I shove those nasty feelings down, swallow hard, and vow not to let it get in the way of helping my friend.

"Let's go home," I say, handing Gracyn her jacket. "We have ice cream, vodka ..." *A clean bathroom in case I need to puke.*

Lis tucks some bills under her pint glass, and we somehow manage to get Gracyn out to my car.

"Gracyn, give me your keys," Lis says, her hand extended, palm up. "Aidan and I can get my car later." Her boyfriend is the stuff that romance novels are made of.

18

Kate

THIS IS NOT LIKE any stomach bug I've ever had before. Sick but not. There but not really.

Queasy.

Icky.

Some days are worse than others, but none of them are ever really *great*.

"Sugar, you doing okay? You don't sound so good," Mama says on an early morning call.

Soft down pillows cradle my head and one foot rests on top of the comforter while the rest of me snuggles deep into the fluffy warmth. If I lie perfectly still, I might be okay. "I'm fine, Mama. Just tired," I croak, my throat dry from sleep.

My mother *tsks* at me. "I hope you didn't catch something from those babies in your class. Drink some juice, take your vitamins, and all that. We can't have you sick when you come home in a couple of weeks."

She's right. My sister-in-law has just stopped puking her guts up from growing baby *número dos*. If I descend on all them and bring any kind of sickness with me, she just might kill me.

"I'll be healthy, I promise," I tell her. "I need to get up and shower, Mama. I'll talk to you later." I end the call and toss my phone to the middle of my bed. *Lord have mercy, I don't feel well.* I roll to my side and breathe through my mouth until the roiling subsides.

As I contemplate making the move to a sitting position, I run through my class roster, making mental notes on who has been sick lately and whether or not they wiped their hands on me or sneezed on me. Anything. I am nothing if not religious with the hand sanitizer for this very reason. I hate being sick.

I push myself up and count to ten. So far, so good. When I stand though, my stomach revolts, and I run to the bathroom, wrapping myself around the cool porcelain just in time to heave. And heave. And heave again.

"Kate, you okay?" Gracyn calls.

She's the second person to ask me that today, and the sun's not even up yet.

"Yep. 'M fine." Actually, I'm seriously starting to question whether or not I really am. I lean back against the tub, the tiled floor cold on my legs.

I tilt my head back and try to relax all the muscles in my core. Breathing carefully. Moving as little as possible. Stillness has become my new best friend. Finally, I pull myself up from the floor and rinse my mouth out, splashing some cool water on my face. I open the cabinet door to pull out a fresh towel and see an array of pads, tampons, all unused since ...

Since when? Christmas? Meh, I was in Mississippi for Christmas and used what I had there.

Side-eyeing myself in the mirror above the sink, I count the weeks since my last period and come up the same each time. It doesn't make sense. Period at Christmas, no sexy times since then, so I can't be ...

Lord, I can't even think the word.

"Coffee's made," Gracyn yells from the hallway.

I'm having a crisis here, and my roommate is yelling about coffee. The faint odor of it invades my senses, and I lurch for the toilet, retching one last time.

No. Nope. No.

I rinse my mouth again and start the shower, hoping the now offensive smell will have dissipated enough by the time I finish up in here to grab a piece of toast from the kitchen. Or a cracker. I don't know.

I know. I totally know.

By the grace of God, I manage to get myself together for work. Opting for a bottle of green tea and a sleeve of plain crackers to get me through the day.

I search my symptoms during rest time, and for the love of all that is good, I don't like what Dr. Google is telling me.

I can't be.

According to my newest enemy, it's entirely possible to

have a period early in pregnancy, which would mean ... I'm—

Nope. I can't be.

I close my laptop and put my head down for a rest, too. Denial and avoidance are my two new best friends. I'm totally ostriching this thing I have going on. This is such a foreign feeling for me. After what went down with Chance, I've made a big damn effort to not stick my head in the sand anymore, to face everything head-on. That saying about leaving nothing to chance, I normally take that shit pretty seriously. But the prospect of this, this situation, scares the shit out of me.

By the time I get home, bypassing McBride's for some much-needed quiet and solitude, my nerves are frayed. I make my way through the apartment, putting things away as I go. My lunch bag in the kitchen, laptop on the coffee table. The peace and sense of order that these simple things usually bring me are nowhere to be found.

Shuffling into my room, I sink down onto my bed and heave out what should be a deep, cleansing breath. Instead, it comes out shakier than I wanted and does nothing to calm me. Not a damn thing.

The need to process—*I can't even bring myself to think the word*—this p-p-predicament without actually talking to someone is overwhelming. And the only person I really want to talk to about any of this is the one person I can't reach. The person who deserves to know before anyone else.

I could text him. But, with his Merry Christmas text being the impersonal brush-off it was, I'm pretty damn sure that, even if I could reach him, this news wouldn't really excite him. Instead, I pull a thick sheet of paper from the stationery box my mama gave me for my last birthday and settle it on the surface, lining it up perfectly parallel with the bottom edge. I run a finger along the slightly bumpy surface, noting the imperfect pattern of fibers in the handmade paper. Anything to avoid what will undoubtedly be a difficult letter for me to write.

Jack,

Lord, how do I even begin this? Remember when I told you we were good, nothing to worry about on the exploding-condom front? Turns out, that might have been a bit premature. I haven't taken a test yet. I'll be honest, I'm not sure I can. I need to sit with it, make peace, process the reality of this ... change in direction. I sure as hell did not think this would happen. I really want you to know that.

You were clear on the fact that a family was not something you planned on having. Your job is your focus, and I get that; I do. But, as scared as I am about being solely responsible for another human being, I'm going to do this. I want to do this. And, when you get back, if you want to share in this little surprise gift, I—we—will scoot on over and make room for you.

Be safe.

—Kate

I STARE at the simple words I scratched onto the paper, wondering what Jack will think when he reads them. If he reads them.

Fully aware that I'm not ready for Gracyn to stumble across this little nugget of information, I carefully fold it and look around my room. My gaze lands on the pile of untouched journals stacked on my bookshelf, the pretty red one from Jack solidly in the middle of the grouping. I ease it from where it sits, realigning the others so that they're centered in size order.

The soft, buttery red leather feels decadent beneath my fingertips. The gift both unexpected and absolutely cherished. I open the cover, careful not to abuse the spine. The cream-colored paper, lightly lined, beckons for words. Pleading to perform a special service. *How can I have seven beautiful journals and no words in them? Is it really marring the pages, to fill them?*

Decision made, I pick up my pen from where I tossed it moments ago and date the top of the first page.

Oops. Such a simple word, but all the holy cows can it be powerful, too! Only by one of the definitions, are you an oops though. A surprise? You know it. But I will never apologize for your existence, nor am I dismayed. I haven't confirmed that you're really there. I'm not quite ready to share you with the world in any capacity just yet. I want to keep you close, just the two of us, since your father isn't here. Lord, your father. I wish I could predict how he'd react to this whole thing, but, baby, I don't know. Whether he's with us or not, you and I are going to have an amazing adventure.

I TUCK my letter to Jack between the pages and set my pen aside. This might possibly be the only way my baby will ever know his or her daddy. The weight of that thought forces me into the stack of pillows at the top of my bed. I clutch the journal to my chest and stare out my window, streetlights casting small pools of light below.

It'll be okay.

I'll be okay.

We ... we'll be okay.

"HEY, WHAT'RE YOU DOING?" Gracyn asks, pulling me from a dream that ghosts as soon as my eyes flutter open. "You still not feeling well?" She leans against the doorframe, not venturing into what could be a sick room.

I don't feel great, but it's not like I'm contagious. "I'm fine, really. Just tired from the little darlings." I tuck my journal under the rumpled blanket on my bed, praying that the cranberry-red cover is somehow hidden under the snowy sea of white linens.

"Mmm, they hit their slump?" she asks, taking a seat in the chair by the window. "Are they acting up?"

Pushing myself up so that I can lean against the head-board, I tilt my head back and forth before answering. "They're somewhere between lawless heathens and full-out riot. The snow days aren't helping much either," I lament. "They need some damn consistency."

Gracyn purses her lips, nodding slowly, but avoids meeting my eyes. "I used to live for snow days," she says softly.

Something's up with her. Or maybe I should say something *more* is up with her.

After the bullshit with her accounting client and the cozy, completely misleading family picture he posted, she has been dealing with misunderstandings, bad timing, and more fallout than a person should ever have to. I know it's hard, with Gavin and his band touring Europe, but her world has completely been thrown ass end up.

"Has Gavin responded to any of your messages?" I ask gently.

Her lip pinched between her thumb and forefinger, she shakes her head.

"You givin' up on him?"

Gracyn snaps her head up, tears sparkling in the corners of her eyes. Her nostrils flare as she tries her best not to fall apart.

19

Kate

"Nope. I'm going to do it," Gracyn says beaming.

I love her, but I'm worried about her. "Gracyn, he hasn't returned a single message. Hasn't texted, sent an e-mail. He hasn't called again. Nothing."

Is this a maternal-instinct kind of thing? When did I become the voice of reason around here?

I drop into my chair and hoist my feet up onto the edge of my bed, sinking low into the cushions. Reflexively, my hands settle low on my belly, and my eyes drift shut. I'm so damn tired.

"Tell me again what you're gettin' inked," I say.

She wants to talk for the first time in a long time, finally opening up a bit again after essentially mourning the loss of her job, walking away from her overbearing asshole of a father, and hearing nothing from Gavin while he was on tour. In fact, it's been a couple of weeks since our last chat, and nothing's really changed except Gracyn is decidedly less weepy and sprawled comfortably across my bed.

"Are you still feeling like shit?" Gracyn asks, eyes taking in where my hands are splayed.

"Nope," I lie. "Just relaxing." I twist the hem of my shirt in my hands, hoping that looks more natural, more chill.

She hums at me, her tell that she thinks I'm lying, but whatever. We're talking about her right now, not me.

"Right. So, you know how Lis went to the last show of the tour? When Aidan took her to Dublin to see his family? She recorded the last song that the band played, the one that hasn't been released."

She's watching me, her gaze skating over me while she talks. I stuff down an after-school yawn and try hard to look like I'm not about to pass out.

"Yep."

"The recording isn't the best, but I'm pretty sure it's the song he was working on in Central Park when he was sere-nading me." Gracyn shifts forward, pushing off of the headboard and scooting her ass to the center of my bed. Thankfully, the more she talks, the more distracted she gets, folding and creasing the fabric of my duvet, making small fan shapes and then smoothing them out again.

"But the words, Kate," she sighs. "The lyrics of that song absolutely speak to my soul. I know how badly I screwed this thing up with Gavin. Every step, right from the very start. That whole twenty-twenty hindsight is making me its bitch, but I want this. It's a way to always have a piece of him close to my heart, you know?"

Do I fucking ever.

"It's the last line of the song. *One kiss, and I was done. Baby, you're my one.* In a simple script, maybe along my rib cage." She sits up straight, running her fingers just underneath her left boob.

Boobs. Mine are popping, big-time. I'm almost exclusively wearing sports bras at this point because it just feels better to have them locked in tight to me. No bounce, no movement. Nothing brushing against them.

"Kate? Did you hear me?" Gracyn asks, head cocked to the side and her eyebrow raised up high. Just the left one.

There's no use in trying to lie. She wants an answer to something, and I have no idea what she asked.

So, I suck it up and admit, "I didn't, sorry. I kind of blanked somewhere after you showed me where you want this permanently etched into your skin. But think about it, G. Tattoos are forever. What if he never speaks to you again? What if there is no forward for the two of you, and then you have to explain having the lyrics of what's inevitably going to be a wildly popular song inked by your heart to some other guy? That's going to be an awkward conversation. I'm just sayin'."

Gracyn's jaw tightens a bit as my words settle between us. "You don't understand, Kate. Your dude was here and gone again. Hell, you didn't even tell us that you were seeing him until well after he was gone." She shakes her head at me, annoyed. "You just enjoyed him and let him go. I know you want more. I know you do. But, until you've met someone and you can't imagine *not* having something of them to hold on to when they're gone, you're just not going to understand."

She pushes herself up off my bed and stalks out of my room. I'm tired and cranky, and I know it, but that was pretty bitchy for someone who has been moping around and making life around her miserable for the past several weeks.

Silence echoes through the apartment after Gracyn leaves, probably heading for McBride's for a shift behind the bar. I'm not sure how much longer she's going to be able to make her half of our rent. Since she walked away from her job, she's been trying to drum up small businesses to do their accounting and working whatever shifts she can get at the Irish pub, but I know money is tight for her. And, now, she's apparently dead set on dropping a chunk of change on a tattoo.

I wouldn't care, but I'm pretty fucking sure I'm going to have some big expenses coming up. I really can't deny it anymore and should probably make an appointment before my belly pops out for real and takes over my silhouette. So much to do. So many things to think about.

Hoisting myself out of the chair, I take my red journal from the drawer beside my bed and grab a pen. The letter to Jack marks the next blank page, about a quarter of the journal filled with everything I want this baby to know about his daddy. With thoughts and concerns about how I'm going to take care of him ... or her and the adventures we'll have. Lists of what I need to buy.

My sweet little Oops.

I'm guessing that, today, you're about the size of a fig. And I still haven't taken an actual test to confirm your existence. You're there though. Changing things up, making yourself known, if only to me still.

Auntie G is maybe losing her mind, but you'll see, when you meet her, that's pretty normal at times. I love her dearly, but today, I just want to string her up by her toes. I've about had enough of her thinking she's the only one dealing with heartbreak and troubles. We've all been there, and maybe— just maybe—she needs to open her eyes and really see what's happening around her. She's going through some things at the moment, so I'm trying to give her some grace.

So, here's your nugget of life advice. Be aware, baby. Your daddy is so good at that. Paying attention to the things going on around him. Observing things, reading people. I don't know if it's something just quintessentially him or if he cultivated it for his job, but he watches, sees things. He's a good man. You've got good genes, baby cakes. Seriously good genes.

EACH ENTRY in the journal reminds me again of all the things that drew me to Jack. All the reasons I took that chance on someone I had known was short-term. The fact that I got a lifelong souvenir from that carnival ride is just a surprise little bonus. One I'll have to tell the world about soon.

Tonight though, I plan on crawling into my fluffy bed

with a big bowl of oatmeal for dinner and a book. I don't have the energy for much of anything else.

In the kitchen, I scroll through Twitter while my oatmeal bubbles and cooks. There's nothing much there aside from the gossip and speculation on how The UnBroken's tour ended. Maybe Gracyn does have reason to be touchy about the shit in her life. There's no escape. No way for her to get away from it since Gavin's disappearance after the last show is all over entertainment news and Twitter.

My issues? I just have to stay away from the world news. And newspapers. And pray that one of my student's family members doesn't run into any problems. Because, if Jake's daddy finds himself in trouble, Jack will be right there in the thick of it as well.

I scoop my steaming oatmeal into a big bowl, sprinkling brown sugar and raisins on top and putting in a dash of cream and shake of cinnamon, and take it to my bedroom. I change into jammies and crawl under the covers. I try to read while eating, but juggling the bowl and holding my Kindle leaves me frustrated, so I give up my book. Not that it was holding my attention, but escaping into another world gives me a much-appreciated reprieve from my thoughts. I seem to be completely stuck on those.

Maybe, instead of grace, I need to give Gracyn some actual space. I have a couple of long weekends coming up, and while I'd still love nothing more than to just skip telling my mama and daddy that I got knocked up, it's something I need to do in person. Face-to-face so that they know I'm really okay and so that I can just face the music and be done.

I stir my dinner and scoop bite after bite into my mouth, savoring the sweetness of the toppings, praying that the starchy goodness will help calm my roiling stomach when morning comes. The spoon clatters in the empty bowl, and though I know it'll be a bitch to clean tomorrow, I set it on my bedside table to deal with in the morning. I make a mental to-do list for tomorrow while checking available flights home for the end of February.

BECAUSE I'VE ADJUSTED MY schedule over the past month or so to accommodate my new, less than fun morning routine, I'm out of the apartment bright and early the next morning. I woke up feeling better than I have in ages and only puked once. Who knew the day would come when I considered that such a win?

Gracyn is still asleep after working until closing at the pub, and that's probably a good thing. I need more than a minute to get myself past the things she said last night. The attitude and shit she's been throwing my way lately.

If I go straight to school though, I'll be crazy early. With a deep, bracing breath, I stop at the drugstore. It's time. I stroll down each aisle, putting an odd collection of items into my basket. Saltines, ginger ale, lemon drops, a pretty new nail polish. Anything to avoid having *just* a pregnancy test as my only purchase.

I pick a box, not giving too much thought to which one I grab. I sure as shit don't need one of the early detection tests. The results are pretty much written in stone, but as I move down the aisle toward the front of the store, I pass through the section of baby things. There are only the basics here, nothing cute and adorable, just the stuff you might grab in an emergency. Diapers, wipes, pacifiers. Teething gel, baby ibuprofen, thermometers. And a rattle.

I pause. A fuzzy lamb with the cutest little face, attached to a minty-blue plastic teething ring, catches my eye. It's absolutely silly, but looking at the items in my basket, it's not like there's any doubt about what's going on in my world. On a whim, I toss the lambikins in with the rest of my crap and get in line to pay. As if the cashier will give a shit.

When I get to school, I tuck the crackers and ginger ale into my lunch bag and the lemon drops and test in my tote. Not a soul is paying attention to me as I waltz through the door as nonchalant as can be. My secret mission, stuffed deep down in the center section of my Mary Poppins bag. I stop in the teachers' lounge on the way to my classroom, thanking God the restroom is completely empty—small favors for being so damn early.

There're no real nerves. No big anticipation. No counting the minutes or fear of turning the test over to read the results.

I know.

I've known for weeks. But seeing those two bright blue lines pop out mere seconds after I cap the end of the stick warms my belly and puts a big-ass smile on my face.

It's official. I'm pregnant.

20

Kate

You know when you do something, thinking you have your poop in a group? And then, at some point in the middle of the whole thing, when it's too late to turn back, you realize you might have made a mistake? Like, maybe I should have made a doctor's appointment before getting on the plane to tell your grandparents about you. Okay, I made the appointment, and I asked if it was okay to fly, but it's not like the doctor has seen us. So, even though the nurse said it was fine, how do I really know that it is? What if I'm ruining you? Lord, I'm already the worst mama in the history of the world.

I bite at the end of my pen as the plane hits a bubble of turbulence and say a little prayer. I'm such a fool. Such an idiot. Barely contained panic pushes me to flip to a fresh page in my journal and apologize to Jack for screwing up our kid. This was so dumb. I should have at least asked Lis; she's a nurse, for Pete's sake. I have a nurse as one of my best friends and didn't ask her a simple question because I'm a fucking idiot.

"Ma'am? Can I get you anything?" A flight attendant crouches down next to my seat.

She hands me a small packet of tissues, and it's only then that I realize I have tears spilling down my face. These hormones are stupid. Because that's got to be the reason for this ridiculous show of emotion.

"Thank you," I say, pulling a tissue from the plastic package. "I'm—I'll be fine. It's just a little ..."

The plane dips again, and my hand drops protectively to my stomach. I haven't puked in almost a week, and it would be a huge step backward if I started again now.

"Maybe a couple of packets of pretzels and some ginger ale," she suggests. "It helped me when I was pregnant." She pats my arm and hurries to the galley at the front of the plane. When she returns a few minutes later, it's with a glass of ice and a green aluminum can in one hand and several packages of pretzels in the other.

"How did you know?" I ask, tearing open one of the tiny snack packs. My stomach churns, but I'm not sure if it's hormones, emotions, or flat-out fear.

What if my father takes one look at me and knows? I need to be able to tell them in my own way. To make them understand that it was nothing but a slip-up and one that I'm already so in love with.

The flight attendant sets the full plastic cup in front of me and says, "I had to work through my pregnancy, and, honey, that turbulence can be a bitch. That look on your face was a permanent fixture on mine for a long time." She taps a nail on my tray next to my cup. "Sip at this while you can. We'll be landing shortly."

"KATELYN, DARLING, YOU LOOK different. Can't tell if you look like you've been sick or if you're filling out a little," my mother says over dinner later.

Neither option makes me feel all that good about myself.

"Thanks, Mama."

"I think you look good with a little meat on you," my father says, patting my hand.

Setting my fork down, I fold my hands in my lap. Now is the time to tell them. "Since y'all seem to be all over how I look and whether I'm sick or not—"

"Hey, we make it in time for dessert?" my brother calls, busting through the back door.

Harper flings herself into my arms, crushing me in her sweet little hug.

"Auntie Kate, I missed you." She kneels on my lap, squishing my face between her palms.

Sam and Jules settle in at the kitchen table, and for a brief moment, I relax, getting lost in catching up with them and all the things going on in their lives.

"It's not convenient with your teaching schedule, but we would love for you to come down if you can. The baby's due in the middle of September. Maybe, if I go early, it could be Labor Day weekend," Jules says.

"Oh, wild horses couldn't keep Katelyn from being here for that baby's birth. Isn't that right?" Mama smiles from the side of her mouth and reaches for my hand. Her gaze finally reaches me, taking in what I'm sure is pure guilt carved across my features. "Kate, baby, are you okay?"

"Darlin'?" The endearment rolls off my daddy's tongue, concern lacing his voice.

And all I can do is nod at my parents. Press my lips together and nod my head like the fool I am for thinking this is all going to be okay.

How am I going to do this? How am I going to have a baby all by myself? How the hell am I going to tell my family that I'm pregnant and the baby's father not only isn't in my life, but I also can't reach him? That I don't know if I'll ever see him again?

"I, um ... I promise I'll do my best but ..." My heart slams against my ribs, and for the first time in my entire life, I'm truly afraid of my family's reaction to my news. Fucking petrified.

How the hell am I going to make this okay? I'm sure my grandma Rose is fixin' to roll over in her grave.

"Auntie Kate, Mimi says you can say anything here 'cause family gonna love you, no matter what." Harper dispensing advice handed down to her from my mama with all the seriousness she can muster shifts my heart right back where it needs to be to get the words out.

"You're right, Harper," I say, smoothing back her curls and pressing my lips to her sweet little forehead. Her lotion, the baby shampoo Jules still uses on her, fills my senses and sets me right. "I might not be able to travel then because, uh ... I have found myself in a similar situation." For some damn reason, talking around the matter and not coming right out and saying it feels like maybe I'm not just talking over Harper's head, but my parents' heads as well.

Sam and Jules are fine. I'm not worried about any kind of judgment from them in the least, but my daddy ...

"What now?" Daddy asks, chin tucked to his chest, eyebrows high as a kite.

"What are you sayin'?" Mama sits straight up in her chair, hands fluttering, twisting her wedding ring around her finger.

Sam snorts, his shoulders shaking with laughter. That boy is always giddy at the slightest possibility of me being the kid in trouble with our 'rents.

Pointing my finger right at Sam, I say, "Just you stop it, you ass."

A giggle bubbles up inside me, threatening to break free regardless of how serious this stupid moment is. Sam's face is bright red, eyes squeezed shut, hands clutching the edge of the kitchen table. It's like time has rolled right on back to when we were kids, and I tried to talk my way out of whatever trouble was coming my way for "washing" Daddy's truck with a steel wool scrubber so that it would be extra clean. I'm in trouble, and my stupid brother can't stop laughing at me.

"Katelyn Hays Beard, you watch your mouth, young lady," Mama admonishes.

Sam and Daddy both mumble, "Brought you into this

world, and I can take you out," and all the stress over telling everybody my news flies away.

My family has never *not* been there for me. Never. There's no way my worst fears will come true. It's another grandbaby, and there is nothing but love in the Beard household for sweet little babies.

"Are you trying to tell us you're ..." Mama nods her head and rolls her hand through the air, not saying the word.

But I can totally understand that because I haven't said it out loud yet either. I sit up straight and fold my hands on the table in front of me. "Actually, Mama, I'm doing my honest best *not* to tell you. But it is true." There's no point in pretending any longer. This is what I came home to do.

"You and Chance are back together?" she asks, looking at me over the top of her glasses. It's her signature *are you tellin' stories* look.

Another laugh surfaces, bubbling up from my toes this time. "Chance is gay," I tell them matter-of-factly. "He was supposed to have told y'all by now. In fact, he told me he was bringing his boyfriend home to meet his parents over Valentine's Day. I take it, that didn't happen?"

My mother looks stunned, but Daddy and Sam just nod, like they've known all along.

"But—"

"He asked me to keep his secret until he broke it to his mama and daddy, but that was supposed to happen ages ago. So, no, Mama, it's not Chance's baby."

"Whose is it?" Daddy grumbles, and I swear, he's shifting his weight to go grab his shotgun. "Where the hell is this new guy, and why haven't we heard anything about him besides the fact that he knocked up my baby girl and isn't man enough to come here with you to tell us about it?" Yeah, his hand is itching to sift through his ammo boxes.

On a deep, bracing breath, I explain that I met him through school.

"So, he's another teacher. What grade?" My mother jumps up, clearing dishes from the table.

I eye the fudge cake she made, hoping she doesn't try to send me to bed without dessert.

"Actually, he was having lunch with one of my kiddos." The cake knife clatters to the counter as my mother whips her head up to gawk at me. "No, no, no. Don't give me that look, Mama. He was home, visiting his nephew—kind of nephew—between deployments and—"

"Deployment? So, he's in the service," my father interrupts, respect lacing his words.

"Yes, sir. Special Forces," I offer. Because, though I know that's impressive, it's really the extent of what I know about his job. "He's in the desert for a couple of more months. I don't know where he'll be after that. He doesn't know about ... this. I can't really reach him," I mumble.

Now that it's out there, now that people know, I wish more than anything that I could talk to Jack. Why didn't we exchange e-mail addresses? At the very least, I could have e-mailed. But how is that any different from texting him? Either way, it's just a message that he'll get, or maybe he won't. Hell, I couldn't even conceive of telling my parents over the phone. I'm a face-to-face girl, for sure. And I'm right back to wondering what I would even say.

The silence in the kitchen is deafening. Even Harper has muffled her usual chattiness, giving me the toddler version of the same appraising look gracing everyone else's faces.

Time stretches interminably, achingly slow.

My heart sinks, and I just want to crawl into bed and cry. The hormone flip that goes along with being pregnant is a bitch. Now that I'm not puking at random moments, I feel like I'm always on the verge of breaking down and crying. Tears burn behind my eyes, and I pull in a shaky breath.

Jules leans over, reaching for my hand. "Are you gonna find out what you're havin', or do you want to be surprised?" she asks.

"You mean, more surprised?" my brother blurts.

And, finally, it's like everyone just resets and comes back to what's important.

"We're going to have two new babies for Christmas," Mama says, a big cheesy grin stretching across her face.

At this, Harper bounces up, running to her mimi. "I gettin' two babies?" she asks, her thumb pressing down on her pinkie.

Mama tucks Harper's ring finger down for her, showing her what two looks like. "Sampson, you need to work with your daughter on her numbers."

After the initial shock wears off and I talk my daddy out of trying to call up Fort Bragg, we get kind of excited.

. . .

MAMA, JULES, AND I spend the rest of my long weekend shopping, looking at all the cutest baby things.

"Well, I think you should find out what you're havin'," Mama declares. "You're a planner, Kate. And, being that you're doing this on your own, you need to be organized. We can't be buyin' pink if we're havin' blue, and Lord knows, we've got to get your nursery goin'." She does that looking-over-the-top-of-her-glasses thing again. I've been getting more than my fair share of that nonsense, but the real issue? "And, honestly, you should just move home, sweetie. There's no better time."

"Not making that decision right now. I've told you that."

New York has become my home, and I really don't want to think about not being able to watch my students grow up and progress. One of my favorite things is having my kiddos from my first year teaching there come in and be reading buddies to the current class. This is the first time that's happened, and it's been just amazing.

"You can still teach here, and I'll get to snuggle both of my new grandbabies. Harper can be my helper. We'll just have a grand ole time."

Lord have mercy, I love my mother, but I'm not sure I can live in the same town as her anymore. Next thing you know, she'll have me moving into my old room.

Like she was reading my thoughts, she continues, "And we can make Sam's old room into the nursery, so the baby is good and close to you."

"Not happenin'. *If* I come back to Hattiesburg, I won't

be movin' back in with you and Daddy," I tell her, flipping through a rack of sleepers. "But that's a big *if.*"

Mama tries several more times, dropping hints, pinning nursery ideas to her Pinterest board, and even leaning on my father for an extra kick of guilt. By the time I get on my plane to head back north, I'm exhausted but feeling more at peace than I have in weeks. Now, I need to spill my shit to Lis and Gracyn.

21

Kate

A LOT CAN HAPPEN in four days. A person can go from being petrified of breaking news to family to making plans for matching monogrammed onesies for Christmas pictures. And your roommate can go from forlorn and downright depressed to getting a tattoo under her boob of lyrics to a song to hooking back up with the man of her dreams.

"And he even said he'd play at McBride's for St. Patrick's Day as long as we don't advertise that it's him. God, he's just so—"

"Not-your-typical rock star," I finish for Gracyn as she flops back on our couch.

"So true." She rolls her head to the side as a yawn rips from my body. "You gonna be there?"

There's no way I can go to the Irish pub on St. Patrick's

Day and *not* drink and have it go unnoticed. "Maybe. I'll try, but I feel pretty behind at school, so—"

Gracyn hits me with a look. I've blown my friends off far too many times in the past couple of weeks; if she didn't have her own hot mess of shit to deal with, she'd be up my butt, demanding to know what was going on with me. As it is, she just seems perplexed, like maybe she's missing something.

"Mmhmm. Hey, did I tell you the potter you fell in love with on your pre-Christmas mountain trip contacted me to do his accounting?"

Thank God for the change of subject. "You didn't. How did he find you?"

Gracyn pushes herself up off the couch and skips across the room toward the hallway. "I guess he's doing the whole small-business thing, rebranding or something. He had Addie do a website, and she referred him on to me. That girl has been a really good addition. We should hang out with her more."

"We should," I agree.

Finn stepped in it when he convinced Addie to give him a chance, not that he didn't have to work damn hard to convince her. But there are no two people more suited for each other.

"You going to bed already?"

It's early for Gracyn, but I feel like I could pass out in a heartbeat.

Not even trying to hide her giddy excitement, Gracyn twirls—freaking twirls—as she inches farther away. "Sort

of. Gavin's in LA for one more night, so we're going to"—
she waves her hands in the air—"chat for a bit."

Her thousand-watt smile lights up the room, and I
couldn't be happier for her. From what she's told me, she
and Gavin have finally found a way to be together. All their
mess is getting worked out, and they are for reals dating
now, actually dating as opposed to the running-away and
then long-distance crap they did.

"Have fun, sweetie. Make good choices," I call.

"*Pffft*. What could happen? Not like we're having reck-
less sex all over the place."

Sometimes, the unexpected just kicks you in the ass.

AND, A MERE HANDFUL of days later, the truth of that
thought darkens the doorstep of McBride's Public House.
The pub owner's death took everyone by surprise. Francie,
the man who selflessly took care of so many, making a
small family of misfits, evidently didn't want to burden
anyone with his illness. Sneaking off for a rest late in the
evening on St. Patrick's Day, he went into his office by the
stockroom. Gracyn was devastated when she found him
hours later, splayed across the floor, already gone.

Francie was known for taking in strays and giving them
a purpose. In fact, until Gracyn walked away from her family's accounting firm and offered to lend him a hand, Francie
only employed young men from Ireland who'd found themselves wandering, in need of a soft place to land. His business model of hot men with a brogue kept the bar full, the

beer flowing, and the drama low. Not that Gracyn amped up any drama when she started tending bar. That was just a matter of Francie's health failing and him needing another set of hands before his favorite holiday. The fact that he passed on the day he did, knowing that he had helped one of his surrogate kids, just made the whole thing even harder.

Aidan might have known Francie the longest, but Finn, Lis, and Gracyn were hit the hardest. Francie was the father each of them had seemed to be missing in life. I didn't have the same relationship with Francie as the others, but they say funerals are not for the dead, but for the living. My friends here have made me feel more welcome, more a part of their tight-knit family than the group I grew up with or even my sorority sisters ever could, and I thought we were close.

"Gracyn, you ready?" I ask softly.

"Not in the least," she replies, sniffling.

The last three tissues pull free at the same time, leaving the box itself to tumble to the counter. I set the empty box in our recycling bin, replacing it with a fresh one.

With my tote bag on the counter, I sift through the contents, adding several travel packs of tissues, mints, and a water bottle. "It's time, G. We need to get going."

"How am I going to do this? I can't say good-bye to him. I just can't," she says, fresh tears thickening her words. "He was more of a father to me in the last couple of months than mine was in the twenty-four years he had. God, Francie was always there for us. How ..."

"I know, babe. Come on. Let's go honor him."

I reach for her hand, pulling her into a hug. Gracyn squeezes me and shuffles out the door of our apartment while I throw on my raincoat, grab one for Gracyn, and sling my tote bag over my arm. I push down the wooziness that seems to be lurking just on the fringe today and slip into the car waiting at the curb.

Gavin turns, extending his hand through the front seats. "Kate, right? Good to finally meet you. Wish it were under different circumstances though."

I shake his hand, noting the way his eyes soften when he glances at Gracyn.

At the cemetery, he hops out of the car and gathers his golden hair back into a perfectly messy bun, one I wish I could accomplish on the regular. The lead guitarist for The UnBroken is gritty and gorgeous onstage, but in a dark suit, he's on an entirely different level. I wonder what Jack would look like in his uniform, rumpled, coming back from a mission. The formal one reserved for special occasions. More and more, I find myself wishing he were really a part of my life and not just a fleeting thing.

We gather at the graveside, each of my friends supported by their person—Gracyn and Gavin, Lis and Aidan, Finn and Addie. And then there's me. I tuck my hands into the pockets of my coat, using the fabric to mask how I splay them across my belly, the need to feel Jack close to me in this moment almost overwhelming.

I've been camouflaging my changing figure. Big sweaters and A-line shirts, leggings and jeans with the top button popped. Hell, I'm a little surprised I was able to get my black dress closed, though I'm sure this will be the last time I can wear it for a while. Thank God funerals are not a common thing in my world. I should be done cooking this kiddo and back to my normal size before I have to do this again.

Thoughts like this—clothes, random things—distract me from the cold, from the sadness. From my utter loneliness.

The world tilts and spins, the ground threatening to rush up at me. I should've eaten something this morning, I know better than to trust the relative newness of not leaving the house with an empty stomach.

Father Callahan lifts his head, meeting my eye as the final strains of "Amazing Grace" float off into the wind, and I can't help feeling like I've been caught doing something wrong. I was raised in the church, not Catholic, but still, I know I should've had my head down, eyes closed. But, the minute I took that stance, I felt ill. Sick and more than a little woozy, but I shoved that shit down because this is not about me. My friends, the family that I've found far from my own, are grieving today. This is their good-bye.

My heart breaks at the loss of Francie McBride, but there is no way—no fucking way—I'm going to steal from him in this moment. Francie was like a father to my friends Lis and Gracyn and especially Finn.

Swallowing my misery, I brace as my stomach does another untimely flip and roll. *Deep breath in, slowly blow it out. Deep inhale, slow release. I'm okay. I can make it through the service, and then I'll go home to bed.*

With tears tracking down her face, Gracyn reaches a hand toward me. I quickly grasp it, giving her a squeeze, thankful for the grounding contact. Caretaker tendencies and distraction come together in that moment, and I dig into my bag, passing out packages of tissues. Anything to keep myself from falling apart as unbidden tears flood my cheeks. I'm not a crier. Never. Not at sad movies, not when I read. I just don't, and today, they just won't stop.

"You okay?" Gracyn asks, leaning in close.

I just nod, afraid to open my mouth because, at this stage, I'm either going to bawl my eyes out—and I'm without a doubt not a pretty crier—or I'm going to hurl. And no one appreciates it when someone pukes at a funeral. That's just bad manners.

"Kate? Honey, you don't look good. Are you going to ..." Lis, a nurse, leans in from my other side, assessing me as the priest continues his homily. Her hands flutter over me, taking my pulse, checking for a fever. "G, get the water bottle from her bag," she directs.

Gracyn rummages through my Mary Poppins bag and pulls out my water bottle, twisting off the lid. I reach for it, taking a tentative sip, praying silently that my nausea doesn't choose this solemn moment to rear its ugly head again.

A chair appears, seemingly out of nowhere, and I sink into it, dropping my head into my hands. "I'm sorry," I mumble, sipping at the water bottle Gracyn thrust into my hands.

Bagpipes keen and groan, their sad melody echoing across green hills. The remnants of an early spring shower chill the air as it swirls around the small crowd gathered on the hillside. When the service is done, when handfuls of dirt have been tossed into the open grave, and the ceme-tery is all but empty, Lis and Gracyn turn to me.

"You going to make a doctor's appointment, or am I going to drag you in?" Gracyn demands. "I know I've been kind of preoccupied lately, but I haven't missed you still feeling like shit. The way it comes and goes, how long has this been going on? Either the kids in your class really are cesspools of germs or you need a little boost to get over this and get healthy again."

"I made one. I'm going in tomorrow—in the morning, I think." In fact, it's at precisely nine in the morning. I prepped my substitute plan as soon as I made the appoint-ment and am finally ready to do this and face the facts.

"Who's the doctor? Do you want me to try to get you in sooner with someone else?" Lis offers. "Or I can go with you. I have the day off."

We've all been so scattered, wrapped up in our own lives lately. I've missed my girls.

I brush more of the never-ending tears away and smile tightly. "I'll be okay, really. You need to sleep in once in a while, loll in bed with your sweet man." I squeeze Lis's hand and nod toward Aidan. "Let him take care of you. I'll let y'all know when I'm done."

I hug Gracyn and say, "I'm going to go. I'll grab an Uber and crawl into bed. Please raise a glass to Francie for me, okay?"

"We will, but let us drop you at home. And I'll bring you a plate from the pub later," she insists. "Gavin, will you grab the car, babe?" She pulls my hand through her elbow, and we walk slowly toward the tree-covered lane that snakes through the cemetery grounds.

As soon as my zipper releases and my dress falls to the floor, all the ickiness I was feeling earlier dissipates. Like the minor constriction around my middle was just way too much. I pull Jack's big, soft T-shirt over my head and slide on flannel PJ pants that are so soft and cozy it's like wearing nothing at all.

It's only late afternoon, but with all the emotion of the day, I crawl into bed, not even bothering with my journal. I'll have all the details tomorrow after my appointment.

22

Kate

I'VE KNOWN DEEP DOWN inside. Of course I've known, but I didn't want to face it because, once you acknowledge something like that, say it out loud, it's real. And this just became all kinds of real.

"Let's just see what we've got here," the nurse says as she moves the wand around on my belly. "We should get good heart sounds since you're thinking maybe your first trimester is up." She poses the statement like there's no question, or maybe it's a touch of judgment. That's not something I'm going to worry about at the moment. I have enough on my plate as it is.

The room fills with a rhythmic whooshing, and there's no question that it's my baby's heartbeat I'm hearing. That's my little Oops, thrumming away. I smile at the nurse, expecting to get the same right back, but as she moves the wand and tilts her head, a bad feeling washes over me.

"That's it, right? That's my baby's heartbeat?" I ask, worry seeping into my voice.

She hums a noncommittal sound and sets the wand on the counter, her mouth a tight line. "I'll just go get the doctor, so she can chat with you." And she's out the door before I have a chance to ask anything further.

Tears sting the backs of my eyes. This is my fault. I drank wine and tequila in the mountains with Jack. I flew home for Christmas and drank my fill there. I have drowned this child in alcohol and bad decisions before it —he? she maybe?—ever had a chance. I should have come in as soon as I suspected I was pregnant. I should have had some kind of maternal inkling that made me make better choices. I should have *something*.

Dr. Delaney walks in, all smiles, and rests a calming hand on my shoulder. "Hey, Kate. Isn't this a surprise?"

"Yeah." I swipe at the gathering tears. "Is everything okay though? We were listening to the heartbeat, and the nurse got real quiet and then didn't say anything other than she was going to get you. Oh my God, did I ruin it? Is my baby okay?" My words come out in a rush, desperation crawling up my spine.

"Let's take a peek, okay?" She pulls over a sonogram machine and squeezes a glob of warm gel on my stomach.

I close my eyes, afraid to look. Petrified by what I'll see, of what she'll say. The same whoosh that I found so exciting a few minutes ago now fills me with dread. There's an echo and a skip, not the solid thump-thump of a well-defined beat.

"Well, there we are," Dr. Delaney singsongs. She chuckles softly, moving the wand, clicking at the attached keyboard. "Looking good, Mama. You're gonna have your hands full in a couple of months. Oh, Kate, honey, open your eyes. Look at your babies."

Babies?

I pop one eye open, afraid to commit fully to looking at the screen. "Oh ..." Hot tears tumble down my face. Babies. Two of them. "There're two?" And that's just proof that there is such a thing as dumb questions because I'm lying here, looking at the tiny little aliens bouncing on the screen.

"Two. Can't tell yet whether they're going to be pink or blue yet, but you've got two healthy-looking babies measuring in right around fifteen weeks, give or take a couple of days." She prints off a stack of pictures and wipes the goo off me, handing me extra paper towels to finish the job.

I put myself back together, only half-listening to what the doctor is saying. *What the hell am I going to do? I can't do twins on my own, can I? Since Gracyn's moving in with Gavin, I'll have the room, but there is so much more to consider, to plan for. I need my planner. I need to sit down and see the schedule for the rest of the school year, figure out what needs to happen when. I need to tell my friends. And I need to cry. Holy shit, what am I going to do?*

"Any other questions?" Dr. Delaney asks, drying her hands and chucking the paper towel into the garbage can.

I look around the room, realizing how much I've missed in the past few minutes. The exam room is tidied up; the nurse has come and gone, leaving a gift bag on the counter by the sonogram pictures; and evidently, I missed an entire conversation as well. My heart sinks when I think that this is why there is supposed to be two parents at these things.

Holy fuck. I'm knocked up. With twins.

Blowing out a deep breath, I blink a few times and say, "I have so many. But I think I need to process this, let it settle in my brain. Can I call the office in a day or so? I, uh … this wasn't planned."

"Absolutely. We'll see you in a month, but call us anytime." She reassuringly squeezes my hand and adds, "Congratulations, Kate. It's going to be fine."

I manage to hold my tears at bay until I'm tucked into my car, the heater running at full blast. Only as I touch the heart of Baby A and then Baby B on the sonogram image do I let the tears fall freely. Once again, life has thrown me for a loop, smacked me upside the head. There is no way past this, but through it. So, I dry my eyes, blow my nose, and send an SOS text, asking Gracyn and Lis to meet me. Gracyn responds that they are both at McBride's.

"HEY." LIS HUGS ME tight. "What did the doctor say? You went today, right?" She holds me at arm's length, taking note of my puffy eyes and red nose. "Oh, Kate, what is it?"

Lis pulls me to a barstool, and Gracyn reaches for my

bottle of tequila, setting it on the bar in front of me. I reach out and place my hands on either side of the bottle.

"It's going to be more than a minute before Mr. Patrón and I spend any quality time together again," I say quietly. If I had my shit together, I'd have done something super Pinteresty to tell these girls that they're going to be aunties. Instead, I release the bottle, bidding it a silent farewell, and reach into my bag.

"Kate"—Gracyn pulls the bottle away from me—"did your sailor knock you up while he was ashore?" Her brows are high, eyes wide.

"He's in the Army," I remind her and set the stack of black-and-white photos on top of the bar.

Gracyn scoops them up, sifting through, handing each one to Lis as she goes. "Oh my God, he did. You're having a baby," she exclaims, cheeks pulled up in a cheesy grin.

"She's having two." Lis looks from the last sonogram picture to me and back again. Sifting through the photos a second time, she sets them down on the bar. "How long have you known?" She fixes me with the same kind of glare that the OB nurse gave me. The one that's assessing and a touch judgy. The one I've been dreading.

"A bit." I spread the pictures apart, pausing on each. Those are my babies.

"Totally makes sense," Gracyn says, placing a glass of water in front of me. "You've been weird, didn't come in for …" Her voice trails off as she looks to the framed black-and-white photo on the wall behind the bar. She sniffs and continues, "I still can't believe he's gone."

I reach for her hand. "Gracyn, I'm so sorry—"

"Nope, not going there right now. We're celebrating babies." She stills and looks at me—like, looks at me hard. Then, slapping both palms on the bar, Gracyn cackles. "Holy shit, you're pregnant."

No shit.

"Have you told …"

"Jack," I offer Lis, feeling bad that my best friends don't know anything about the man who changed my world. I shrug, continuing, "I can't. He's deployed."

"FaceTime? E-mail? He doesn't have an international phone?" Gracyn asks. "Gavin called from somewhere over there when he was on tour."

"It was a fling, short-term. Surely, you of all people understand that." I look pointedly at Gracyn.

Gavin was her spring break fling. And they went their separate ways, no contact until they ran into each other a year and a half later.

"But you met him at school, right?" Lis pipes in. "His nephew? Or friend's kiddo is in your class? Can you get ahold of him that way?"

I pick up the picture with both babies, the one that has their little alien bodies in profile. "They're Special Forces. Communication isn't really an option. Jake and his mom hardly ever get to talk to Tripp. God, and the last thing I want to do is have his best friend's wife know before he does. That's just too much drama and shit."

Gracyn pushes my water glass toward me. "You're not going to be hiding that for long. Especially not if there're two in there."

She's right. She's totally right, but I don't even know if

Jack told Jake's dad that we were seeing each other. I asked him not to, to keep things quiet, and I just assumed he would. Why, if this was just a hookup while he was on leave, would Jack have told anyone?

"I don't know. I can't think about that right now. I need to process this. Go home and figure out what to do. Are you staying with Gavin tonight, G?"

"I don't have to. Do you want me to come home?"

I shake my head. "No, you're good. Spend time licking your man's tattoos. I'm going to bed early anyway, I apparently am growing a couple of humans." *Jesus, that sounds ridiculous when I say it out loud.* "Thanks, y'all. I, um ... I don't know what I'd do without you." I hug Lis and lean over the bar for Hollywood cheek kisses with Gracyn. "Love you."

I slide off the barstool and safely tuck the stack of pictures into my bag. As I toss a wave over my shoulder, the exhaustion hits. I drag my ass home, and as soon as I can, I crawl under the covers.

I click on the television and flip through the channels before turning it off again. There is no joy in reality TV, cooking shows, or watching people hunt for their dream homes. And I absolutely can't watch the news. Past attempts had me hyperventilating at the slightest mention of American troops.

Instead, I pull out my journal and smooth it across my bended knees. I hope that Jack will want to experience this pregnancy with me, but for now, this is the best I can do.

Flipping the creamy red leather cover open, I find the

next blank page and grab a colored pen—dark purple for today's entry. Nothing like color-coding my feelings.

I wasn't just a little bit wrong. Darlin', I was way wrong. Went to the doctor today because Lis had insisted, and really, it was time. Hell, I wasn't even fooling myself anymore. And surprise, surprise, I'm pregnant. Yeah, that's on me.

Itty-bitty condoms were no use with your big, stupid dick, but I'm telling you, Jack, I sure as shit didn't see this coming. Twins, friend. Twins. Did they hit you with radiation or something to give you super sperm? Is that a government secret? Super-soldier stuff? You're my very own Captain America.

Lis thinks I should try to reach you through Chloe, but ... I don't know ... it feels wrong. Like a breach of trust or something.

I have pictures, Jack. Two little alien babies. The doctor marked them Baby A and Baby B. Since I've been calling the possibility of one Oops, I'm just going to go ahead and bless the extra with the name Uh-Oh. Next visit, they should be able to tell me whether they are pink or blue.

Sweet baby Jesus, we're having twins.

23

Kate

I'M DOING THINGS OUT of order, and that bugs the shit out of me. But I guess I've done this whole thing backward, and Mrs. Altman, my school's principal, was nothing but supportive when I told her what was going on. I mean, I did skate around plenty of the finer details, but those stories really are best kept quiet, shared only with my closest friends, if at all. Poor Lis would probably be horrified if she heard about trying to get that busted condom off of Jack. No, that's probably a story not to tell.

"What's the news? It feels like it's been forever since we chatted. You doing okay?" Jenny asks as I shut Mrs. Altman's office door behind me.

Suddenly, I feel the weight of the world on my shoulders, and I slump into the plush office chair usually reserved for the moms who volunteer in the front office. "It has been a while, more than a minute." I pause, knowing

I'll confide at least a little bit in Jenny. The question is, how much do I tell her?

She's one of the few people in my life who has actually met Jack. And, because she's got her finger on the pulse of everything that happens in this school, she also knows that he's tied to Jake and his family.

"As far as news is concerned—"

"I'm so sorry, Kate. I heard about that nice man who owned the pub you and your friends hang out at." Jenny pats my knee, continuing, "My aunt Louise and her friends go there after they do their thing at the community center —some computer class or tai chi or something. For a while, I thought one of the ladies might have had a thing for the owner, but turns out, they all had a bit of a crush on one of the bartenders."

I chuckle, thinking on all the ladies, young and not, who have had a crush on that bartender because, really, it can only be one to whom she's referring. "Mmm, Finn has quite the following, but, yeah, Francie was a shock. One of many in the past month or so."

Jenny pushes back from her desk and cocks her head, brows drawn together as she waits for me to continue.

"I just told Mrs. Altman, so it's, um, not really a secret anymore, but ..."

"Oh, Kate, you're not leaving us, are you?" she asks, palm pressed to her chest.

There's time to make that decision, so I don't really have an answer for her question. "I don't think so. But ..." I pause, feeling all kinds of self-conscious once again. "Well, I'm, uh ... pregnant," I say quietly, bracing for her reaction.

And bless her, Jenny shows no shock, no judgment. Nothing other than a genuinely excited smile lights up her features. "Oh, sweet girl. Well, that is exciting news. Maybe a bit unexpected?" she asks.

"Yeah, it is. For such a planner, I didn't really see this coming."

"A baby is wonderful. You'll do great, I'm sure. When are you due? Do I know the lucky man?"

And isn't that the million-dollar question?

I heave out a sigh and flop back into the chair, poking lightly at my pooch. "Actually, it's twins, double trouble, so early September but probably more likely to be August. It's going to be a big, hot summer." I huff out a laugh. "Bathing suit season might just be a no-go for me this year."

"Didn't answer my other question." Jenny side-eyes me, eyebrows raised. If she tilted her chin down just a little bit, she'd have my mama's look down to a T.

"You might have met him," I tell her, biting at the inside of my cheek. "It's Jack, little Jake Triplett's uncle. But, Jenny, I have no way of reaching him. I don't think Jake's mom knows we were seeing each other, so that would really be overesteppin' the whole parent-teacher relationship. God, imagine me asking her to let Jack know that I'm knocked up. I just can't."

She nods because, really, that conversation would be awkward as fuck. "He's coming back here though, right? You're going to see each other when he gets back home again?"

I push myself up out of the chair and round the counter that acts as her command post. "I don't know. We didn't really make plans. Sure as hell didn't expect to *have* to see each other. So, I've got to be ready to do this parenting thing on my own. Even if he does show up back here, this"—I sweep my hands up and down myself— "might not be what he wants. You know what I mean?"

Jenny purses her lips, sympathy written all over her face.

I smile weakly making my way to the door leading out to the hallway. "I've gotta get to class now. See you later, gator."

GRACYN: McBride's tonight. Dinner and I'll buy you a Shirley Temple.

Me: Sweet of you to offer. I'm tired though.

Gracyn: You're always tired. We have plans to make, things to discuss.

I am tired all the time. Apparently, growing multiple humans takes a lot out of a person. Who knew? My lesson plans for the rest of the month are done, and the framework for what we need to do through the end of the school year is in place. I really have no reason to use work as an excuse not to go.

Gracyn: Stop running through your to-do list, looking for a reason to just go home, and come meet us. Please?

Gracyn: Chicken tenders with hot sauce and extra ranch …

Gracyn: You know how the babies feel about hot sauce.

Me: Fine.

Watery late afternoon sun filters through the blinds, casting shadows across the pages of my journal. It seems like things are moving superfast now that my pregnancy is out in the open and everyone knows. Everyone, except the man who should. I stare at the page, not quite halfway through the book, where my words hang, mid-thought. For someone who never wanted to mar the inside of a pristine journal so full of promise, I have poured my heart out over these pages. Thoughts and feelings. And my fears, so damn many fears. If Jack comes back and wants the play-by-play of the months he was gone, I've got them. If he decides not to be part of our lives, then my babies will at the very least have a glimpse into who their father was and why I found myself falling for him.

How did that even happen? Do I even know him well enough to have fallen?

Suddenly annoyed with myself and my melancholy thoughts, I close the leather book and tuck it into my tote, locking my classroom as I go.

"So, what are we discussing and planning?" I ask, hanging my tote from the hook underneath the bar at McBride's. "And shouldn't my food be waiting for me already? These kids are demanding little boogers," I tease, hoisting myself into the seat next to Gracyn.

She's set up at the corner of the bar. A notebook in front of her, laptop open as she scrolls through Pinterest.

Kieran sets a coaster on the scarred wooden surface in front of me and reaches for a shot glass and well tequila, not saying a word. He was Francie's last hired McBride's boy, and none of us can quite figure him out. He's the least talkative bartender, and he never really seems to be fully aware of what's going on around him.

"Shit, Kieran, stop with that. She's pregnant," Gracyn says, putting her hand over the shot glasses.

He looks up, wild blond curls tumbling into his eyes as his gaze bounces back and forth between the two of us. "Is she? So, the whiskey then?"

I can't help but laugh at his cluelessness. "No, just soda water and a couple of orange slices, thanks."

He shrugs and makes my drink before walking to the other end of the bar, his attention fully focused on his phone.

"I'm not sure I want to eat here if he's the one doing the cooking," I whisper, leaning into Gracyn.

"No shit." She angles her laptop toward me. "You look through this, and I'll go make us some food. Lis and Addie should be here in a little bit." She hops off her barstool, bussing tables as she makes her way to the kitchen.

Images of baby shower themes fill the screen of her computer, her Pinterest board ranging from extravagant Paris and Eiffel Tower–themed parties to sweet and simple. She even pinned an over-the-top Army theme that looks more like the birthday party of any little boy's dreams.

"She's got you picking your party decor?" Addie asks, perching on the seat just around the bar's corner. Her green hair, a St. Patrick's Day tradition since she and Finn started dating, is tied back from her face, all 1940s pinup style, purple cat-eye glasses perched on the bridge of her nose.

"Apparently. How are you doing?"

I lean over to greet her before remembering she's not a hugger. She gives me a tight smile, lips quirked up in an uncomfortable smirk.

"Sorry, I forgot," I offer.

"You're fine." Her eyes drop to my belly and then dart back up to mine. "What was that?"

"You can see it?" I ask, my fingers drawing lazy circles over where I felt a kick and a push.

Addie pulls her glasses off, setting them on the bar. "I thought I saw something, but ... holy shit," she exclaims, her mouth hanging open in surprise.

This is kind of new, like the next stage of an adventure. And Addie—who is normally so reserved, so closed off—has her fingers twitching, almost reaching toward the side of my belly.

"Wanna see if you can feel 'em?" I press in where somebody just pushed out to see if it'll happen again.

Casting off her reserve, Addie scoots closer and tentatively places her small hand near my bump. I pull her in, and seconds later, we're both rewarded with a strong thump, followed by a skittering push.

Addie lifts her head and takes her hand away. "That's just crazy kinds of weird," she says, sliding back into her seat.

"Let me feel." Gracyn comes dancing across the room, hands out, fingers wiggling.

Lis comes in through the back door of the pub, baskets

of food clutched in her hands and balanced precariously along her arm. "They're moving?" she asks, hastily dropping the plastic baskets to the bartop.

And, suddenly, hands are all over me, pushing, pressing. Promises and bribes whispered, begging for just one feel.

"Come on, babies. Auntie G will buy you all the pretty pink things that your mama says no to. A pony. The biggest dollhouse ever," Gracyn cajoles.

"No to the pony unless you keep that at your house. Y'all have room for it out there," I say, trying to mimic my mother's mom look. "But I happen to think there's nothing more handsome than men who wear pink."

Don't I know how to throw a hush over a room? I have had a lot of practice with it lately, but I swear, the entire pub goes silent, not just our little group of belly-gropers.

"Did you say men?"

"You're having boys?" Lis and Gracyn ask simultaneously. Eyes wide and bright.

A laugh rips from me as these two crazy girls pull money from their pockets and toss five-dollar bills at Addie.

"Y'all bet on my babies' sex?" I ask, pushing at whichever baby is on my right, shifting him into a better spot. "Assholes." I sit up straight, grabbing for the basket piled highest with food. I load hot sauce and ranch on a piece of chicken because, when my boys decide they're hungry, they mean it.

Gracyn spins her laptop to face her and deletes more than half of the pictures she had pinned. "That narrows down our party options," she mutters. "How are we decorating our nursery? All kinds of blue, whales and sailboats —how cute would that be?" She taps away at the keyboard, probably making a new board for nurseries.

"Slow your roll, G. We've got time." I push back, needing another drink and to visit the restroom, all at the same time. Pregnancy really is weird.

Lis looks up from her phone where she's been texting almost nonstop since tossing her money across the bar at Addie. "You think that, but it's going to go fast. Those boys'll be here before you know it."

24

Kate

SPRING CONFERENCES ARE ANOTHER round of baring my soul and putting myself out there for the world. But the judgment and questions I expected are nowhere to be found. Every single parent of my students is nothing but supportive and genuinely excited for me. More than a few voice concerns that I'll be done with teaching and choose to stay at home with my boys. But the conference I'm most worried about is with Chloe Triplett.

Of course, she walks in, wearing a bright smile and carrying a blue gift bag. "Hey, I hear we have some exciting news," she trills. "Amelia's mom called me last night and told me you're having twin boys. I hope that's all right."

"Absolutely, we do. Well, I'm excited at the very least." I smile tentatively because this is usually the make-or-break moment with the parents. Although, with the way Chloe is practically pulling books and goodies out of her gift bag, I think we'll be okay.

"Look at you! God, I'd hoped when Tripp was home over Christmas ..." She pauses, letting her wish go unsaid. "But we've got time. He'll be home this summer, and then maybe Jake'll get a sibling. He's been begging for one, but I don't think he gets that he won't be the main man then."

Guilt bites at my heart. She's married, and she was trying, wanting to get pregnant while her husband was home, but it didn't happen. I had a couple of wild nights of sex with a man I hardly knew, and I've got more than I can handle. *Maybe.*

I shove my thoughts away and reach across, squeezing Chloe's hand. "He'll make a great big brother."

"He will, right? Such a little helper. Oh, do the kids know? Jake hasn't said anything to me, and he's usually all over anything that has to do with your happenings."

"Oh my word, no. I wanted to make sure all the parents were informed first and answer any questions. Make sure that we're all on the same page. So, if there is anything you want to ask me, now's the time." My words tumble from my mouth just as they have for every other conference I've had with the parents of my students.

And, when Chloe purses her lips and looks up to the left, I brace myself.

She starts and stops her inquiry, her mouth doing the fish thing over and over again. Finally, Chloe asks, "Do I ... is it ..." She laughs and shakes her head before continuing, "You'll let me know if you need anything, right? Help in the classroom, anything?"

It doesn't take a rocket scientist to figure out that that's not what she wanted to ask. I think the same thing has happened in more than half of my meetings, and I get it. Everyone loves a bit of gossip, information that's pointless but a tad bit illicit. But, when it's Chloe—someone with close ties to Jack—hinting at asking who the baby daddy is, it feels different. Like I'm straddling the line of lying by omission.

Lis's suggestion of getting a message to Jack through Chloe rattles around the edge of my mind as Chloe and I discuss Jake and his classroom performance. That little boy is so ready for advancement to first grade.

Should I ask her about Jack? Ask her to have him contact me when or if he can? It would be wrong. I know in my heart that it would be wrong to ask her to relay a message like this.

I'm stuck though. If she tells her husband and he gossips to Jack, the results could be disastrous. He could think I lied to him at Christmas about being in the clear. He could think I'm somehow trying to trap him. He could just not give a shit, and that might be the hardest option for me to consider. That he just wouldn't care.

"So, don't say anything to Jake, but there's a chance his dad will be able to make it to kindergarten graduation," Chloe shares.

My eyes about pop out of my head, and there's no hiding my shock. At least, I think there isn't, but Chloe rolls right on, ignoring my freak-out.

"You're kidding. Really? That's amazing. I'm so happy for y'all," I gush. "Their deployment'll be done and all?"

More than anything in this moment, I want to ask a million and one questions. Beg her for details and if Jack is coming, too.

Beaming wildly, Chloe nods, her face alight. "Should be. I'm just keeping my fingers crossed and saying all my prayers that everything works out. With any luck, Jake's uncle might be convinced to come, too. Lord, that little boy's head would about explode."

His and mine both.

Later, when I'm settled into my bed, the need to talk to Jack is strong. So, I do the only thing I can in the moment and flip my journal open to the next blank page and pour out my thoughts and emotions.

Jack,

Please know that my heart is torn on what I should've done today. Part of me wanted so badly to ask Chloe to have you call me as soon as you were able. Part of me wanted to beg her not to say a word to her husband because I can only imagine how news like this might be received.

Now ... now it's just a matter of waiting and seeing. Will you come home with Tripp again? I know Jake and his parents are a huge part of your life—like family—but Lord, I would love to be the one to tell you face-to-face. To introduce you to your boys—or at least, the idea of them.

Be safe until you're back on US soil.

"KATE, I'VE INVITED YOUR mother and sister-in-law to your shower, but I haven't heard back from them. Do you know if they're planning on coming?" Lis asks. "Maybe we should have held off until after the school year was done? Everyone seems so busy right now." Her brows push together, concern pinching at her features.

"Are you serious? I know Jules hates that she can't make it, but Mama hasn't responded yet?" I'm shocked at her avoidance.

"Nope," Gracyn says, popping that P.

"Hang on and let me call her." I dial my mama and count as the rings stack up.

When I'm about ready to give up and call the house phone, she answers, "Kate, baby, you doin' all right? Everything okay with my grandbabies?" She's out of breath, and I can hear Harper singing in the background.

"We're fine, but Lis and Gracyn just told me they haven't gotten your RSVP yet. So, I guess I need to ask you if you're doing okay." I don't bother to hide any of the sass in my tone.

"Well, I'm not sure what bee has gotten in your bonnet, but I certainly don't appreciate that—"

"I know, but I've got your attention now, so how about you tell me why you're not coming to my shower?" I might never perfect her mom look, but I sure as hell can rock the teacher voice, even with my own mother.

Silence stretches between us, and I check the screen of my phone, concerned that I've lost her.

"Mama?"

"Is it too much to ask, wanting my baby girl to come home? To have my grandbabies here by family?" Tears touch the edges of her words.

"Of course not, Mama. There's no harm in asking and wanting, but just come to my party. Come meet my friends, see where I live. See my life outside of Mississippi. I promise you won't have to give up your Southern roots if you cross the Mason-Dixon Line for a visit." I hold my breath, replaying the words I just uttered. Hoping and wanting for her to give New York a chance.

Mama concedes.

Two weeks later, when she finally comes to New York for the babies' shower, the chatter begins almost the minute she gets off the plane.

"Now, your daddy and I are buying your cribs, but we'll just have them delivered down home. Don't want to have to pay to move those if we don't have to. And I brought an extra suitcase with me, so I can just pack that full of gifts and take them home with me instead of botherin' with shippin'."

I'm fighting a losing battle with her, but I calmly remind her, "I'm not positive I'm leaving New York, Mama."

She laughs at the idea. "Don't be silly, Kate. You're gonna need help and a lot of it. You think you can schedule and organize these babies into submission? I don't think so, darlin'."

I let her prattle on, not interested in starting anything with her. I'll just let her know—along with everyone else

—when I've made up my mind. In the meantime, I take her to as many places as I can that show her why I love it here so much. And how hard of a decision staying or going will be for me to make.

25

Jack

I'M GOING TO BE late. I knew it was a long shot when I changed my flight at the last minute, but I just couldn't miss out on Jake's kindergarten graduation. Tripp had talked nonstop for the past two weeks about nothing but getting to make it back in time for the big ceremony. I'd had no plans to go back to Beekman Hills. None, but after rolling around in the desert for another six months, spending a few days with my favorite kid sounds pretty good. And the possibility of seeing his favorite teacher and mine doesn't suck in the least.

I throw my rental into one of the only available parking spaces in the elementary school's lot and hustle for the front door at a brisk jog. Once in the building, I follow the little mortarboard clings lining the floor to the cafeteria. Gone are the cramped torture device tables that I squeezed my ass into back in November, and in their place are row upon row of folding chairs.

Parents and grandparents corral squirmy siblings, claiming as much real estate as they can get away with. I search the sea of spectators for Chloe's curly black hair and Tripp's all-too-familiar head. I've been staring at the back of his block head for fucking months. I should be able to immediately find it, but Chloe is alone, an empty seat next to her.

I settle against the back wall, and before long, the principal climbs the steps to the stage.

"Welcome, family and friends. Thank you for joining us this evening as we celebrate the advancement of this year's kindergarten class to first grade. The entire class will perform two musical numbers that they've worked very hard on. Then, each teacher will present their students in turn. Refreshments will be available in the commons afterward. Please allow me to present you with this year's kindergarten class."

One by one, the kids file into the cafeteria and up onto risers set up on the stage. The teachers arrange and adjust them, grouping them by class. I run a hand over my stubble, eyes trained on the entrance. Waiting for a glimpse of blonde waves and a bright smile leading in the final class. I can practically see the sway of her hips as she led the kids down to her classroom that first day, hear the staccato click of those sexy-as-shit heels she was wearing.

The wavy hair and brilliant smile are there, but when Kate lumbers up the stairs, my breath slams out of my lungs in a whoosh. *Fuck me.* Gone is her hourglass figure.

In its place is more of a Violet Beauregarde—after she turned into a blueberry in *Willy Wonka*.

Pregnant. Really fucking pregnant. Honest to God, she looks like she's ready to burst.

My nostrils flare as air forces its way in and out of my lungs. Because I'm no expert, but if she's that fucking pregnant, that means she was already knocked up when we were together. And she likely knew it.

I push off the wall and stalk toward the exit, escape my singular focus. The need to get away driving me out of this place.

"Uncle Jack!" Jake screeches.

The excitement in his voice is the only thing that can stop me in this moment.

Every face in the room turns to look at me. Every single one. Kate leans in, whispering to Jake and getting him settled back into his spot onstage. But, as she descends the stairs, she finds me. Eyes wide, one hand supporting her protruding belly. She's white as a ghost, and she sways slightly as she joins the other teachers kneeling—fucking kneeling—on the hard floor in front of the stage.

Jaw tight, I survey the room, and Chloe pins me with a glare, waving to me.

"Get over here," she whisper-shouts, insisting that I take the empty seat I know is for Tripp.

My head is spinning. My heart pounding against my ribs. *How the fuck did this happen to me again?* I must be a fucking magnet for crazy women looking to start a family. I don't want that shit. Fine for others, but this fucking mess is not for me.

The music starts, and kids begin to sing.

Chloe leans into me again. "Where's Tripp? He said he was getting in before you and—hell, I didn't even know until yesterday that you were thinking of coming to this," she whispers.

"Last-minute decision. He should be here. Flight got in almost an hour before mine," I tell her, getting shushed by the lady behind us. I lower my voice, biting out, "Jake's teacher's changed since fall."

"You met her?"

"Had lunch with Jake a time or two. Sure as fuck didn't know she was knocked up," I grumble.

A hand lands on my shoulder with a hissed admonishment from the dad behind us. "Hey, watch it. There are kids around."

He's right. I mumble my apology and turn back to Chloe, who's using her all-knowing mom stare on me. My phone buzzes in my pocket, giving me the perfect excuse to break eye contact. It's not a number I recognize, and no one knows I'm stateside yet, so I decline the call and focus on the kids singing—shouting—mostly off tune.

"Was it just lunch?" Chloe asks, digging at shit I'm not discussing.

I nod toward the front of the room. "Your kid is doing big things. Stop gossiping."

Chloe settles back in her seat with a huff but side-eyes me every so often. Fully focused on the end of the last song, I lock it down and ignore her. Maybe Jake'll run to us after this shit is done, and we can shuffle out the back. Not sure that I want to come face-to-face with Miss Katelyn

Beard. The conversation we need to have sure as fuck is not appropriate for any kind of audience, let alone with kids around.

My phone buzzes again, and I silence it. There's still no text from Tripp. No call, nothing telling me he got delayed somehow. *Did he miss his connection? Get held up in customs?* Another buzz that is not my friend calling with excuses, so I decline again and turn off notifications for the next hour, sliding my phone back into my pocket. I'm here to see Jake graduate from kindergarten and maybe take him out for ice cream, so when his father finally gets his ass to town, Tripp and Chloe can have a few quiet moments. Yeah, totally gonna run interference with my little wingman, so my buddy can get reacquainted with his wife. My plans of hooking up with the hot teacher are obviously going nowhere.

My ass falls asleep as the eighty-plus kids wearing blue paper mortarboards make their way across the stage to shake hands with their teacher and the school principal. No doubt the scrolls they're handed will end up creased, twisted messes, probably forgotten under their chairs. And, through the whole thing, I can't take my eyes off Kate.

Much as I'm pissed at being played, I can't deny that she looks amazing like that, all swollen, round belly. You'd think, with her so close to dropping the kid, the dude who knocked her up would at least be here in case all this excitement sent her into labor. But I don't see that. No one sitting with her, no one looking concerned. No one to help her up the four steps to the stage when it's her turn to shake little hands.

"She looks like she could have that kid any minute now. Should she even be here?" I ask Chloe, forgetting my earlier avoidance of the subject.

Chloe pulls her phone out, ready to take pictures when we get a little further into the class roster. "Three more months," is all she says, scooting out of her seat and duck-walking toward the front of the room to capture the big moment.

Three more months?

I'm not a doctor by any means, and I have shit for med training beyond basic field first aid, but there's no way in hell Kate's got another three months. She's huge.

Jake walks across the stage, getting his diploma, shaking hands like a boss. But, like the sensitive little dude he is, he places a hand on Kate's protruding stomach and gasps suddenly.

It almost sounds like he said, "They moved!"

Kate laughs and tousles his hair, sending him on his way. And, now, every kid after him wants to feel what he did. Six more hands stop on her belly, and by the time her class is done, she looks relieved to lower herself into the principal's chair onstage for the closing remarks.

Chloe slips back into the seat beside me, sliding her phone back into her bag. "How sweet was that? He's been asking for a little brother or sister again ever since Miss Beard started showing." A smile pulls at her lips, and she adds, winking, "Glad you guys are home for a bit. Tripp's got some work to do." Chloe stands with every other person in the room and claps as the kids are led out in barely contained chaos.

"Where's he going?" I ask, sure that we would just be able to grab Jake and run.

"Refreshments, Jack. Come on. You can't deny that boy the spoils of his accomplishments. Those are special Oreos out there in the commons. Not at all like the ones we have sitting in the pantry at home."

She pulls me up and drags me with her as we fight our way out to the open area just inside the front doors of the school. Tables with bowls of punch and platters of cookies have magically appeared while we were enjoying the ceremony.

"Good to see you again, Captain Jackson," a familiar woman says, squeezing my forearm.

Pretty sure she works in the office, but ...

"Jenny Simpson. I work up front. Kept hoping to see you pop in to have lunch with Miss Beard again, but she said you work with Jake Triplett's dad. So, I figured it might be a while before we saw you again. Welcome back."

She scurries off to help serve punch, and Chloe pins me with a hard look.

"Just lunch?" she asks, snorting out a little huff of judgment.

"Don't start with me," I tell her. "Can we just get Jake and go? I'll buy ten packages of Oreos and all the fruit punch he can handle if we can bolt." I'm not ready to deal with the questions, the looks from Chloe, and I sure as shit am not ready to talk to Kate.

But the universe is not on my side tonight.

Jake worms his way to us, breaking away from his little

friends and runs straight for me. "Uncle Jack, you made it! I didn't know you were gonna be here. Did you bring my dad? Mom, where's Daddy? I thought he was coming. Uncle Jack, come on." His words all run together, questions melding into statements, as he grabs my hand and pulls me toward where his classmates are all sitting on the floor with their treats. Straight toward his ridiculously pregnant teacher. "Miss Beard, look. It's my uncle Jack." He bounces on his toes. "Uncle Jack, she has babies in her tummy."

"I see that." Because what the fuck else am I supposed to say?

Here I was, feeling like shit while out on mission, thinking about her and wondering for the first time in forever if maybe I could give the relationship thing a shot. See if it wouldn't be so terrible to have someone to come home to after deployments. Entertaining the idea of love because that was what I'd thought was happening when I left. That I was falling in love with her. And, all the time we were fucking, she was already knocked up.

Fuck my life.

Kate offers me a tight smile and says, "Hey. How are you?"

Yeah, she's displaying all the textbook signs of lying and withholding information. Shifting her weight and fidgeting, unable to hold eye contact.

I shake my head and answer, "I'm good. You, uh … you've changed."

I take her in from head to toe, dick move on my part because, obviously, she's changed, and I'm just being an ass about it. But, for fuck's sake, maybe I've earned the right to be a little bit of a dick right now.

"Yeah, um ... maybe this isn't the best time, but I'd like to talk to you soon. Maybe we can grab lunch this week if you're around?"

I don't get the chance to answer her.

"Jack." Chloe's voice wobbles from beside me. All the color has drained from her face, tears gathering in her eyes, phone clutched tightly in her hand. "He's gone. Jack, he's gone. The police ... they were calling you, but ..."

"Can you—" I ask Kate, darting my eyes to Jake.

Hand over her mouth, she nods quickly, and I guide Chloe out the front doors of the school.

"What happened, Chloe?"

She trembles, tears finally tumbling down her cheeks. "He stopped at a gas station, walked into a robbery. They stabbed him, took his wallet, and left. Crashed the car. Rental papers. Tried to call you. Why did they call you and not me? Why didn't they call me? He's dead. Oh my God, why?" Chloe crumbles, and I have to lunge to catch her before she hits the ground.

Motherfucker.

26

Kate

"Miss Beard? Why's my mom crying?" Jake asks softly, slipping his hand into mine.

I take a deep breath—at least as deep as I can with these two monsters taking up way too much space in my body. "I don't know, buddy. But I'm wondering if you'd like to be my helper for a little bit. Think you can keep an eye on this very important basket for me while I go get a chair?"

"Are the babies making you tired?" He places his small hand on the side of my belly and waits.

The kiddos love it when the babies are giving high fives, and it seems like that's been happening nonstop these days.

Another deep-ish breath because, if truth be told, growing babies is hard work, and I really am exhausted.

"They are wearing me out, Jake. I'll be right back with a chair and—"

Just then, Jenny Simpson rolls one of the office chairs over, a smile brightening her already-cheery face.

"Thank you, Jenny."

"You know it. Got to take care of you, though it'll calm down a bit with school out for the summer. You know what your plans are yet for next year?" she asks. Lowering her voice, she adds, "I did see that Captain Jackson is back in town."

So did I, Jenny. So did I.

"Where'd he go? I thought I saw him heading this way."

"He stepped out with Jake's mom for a minute." I lean in, whispering, "I think something's happened. She looked like someone stepped on her grave. Do you think you could pop outside and see if they need anything?"

Jenny glances at Jake and then back to me. Plastering on her *it's all going to be fine* smile, she nods once. "I'll be back in a jiff. You go sit down though. You look like you could collapse."

I'm starting to feel like I could, too. I lower myself into the chair with an *oomph*, grateful for the plush office chair as opposed to the hard plastic one I was going to grab from the cafeteria.

Little by little, parents come by to collect their kiddos and thank me for the year. Jake helps me hand out certificates and small gifts to each of the kids. They grow up so much in kindergarten. Not just learning to read and write, but also how to be in a classroom and work with others.

Their little minds are like sponges, soaking up every experience, every nugget of knowledge.

"Is one of those for me?" Jake asks, yawning as he hands over another little bags of goodies.

"Absolutely. Are you getting tired, buddy?"

Jack and Chloe have been gone for well more than a hot minute, and Jenny has yet to come back from checking on them. In fact, the last of my parents have come for their kids, and when I look up, the commons area is just about empty. Only a handful of teachers, volunteers, and the custodial staff.

Jake leans hard on my chair and rests his head on my shoulder. "When is my mom coming back for me?" he whines.

I have never once heard this child whine in the nine months that I've had him in my class. Whatever happened, it must be serious because Chloe Triplett is always here for her kiddo. *Always.*

I run through the short list of things that I planned to do tonight before leaving and decide that I can push them all off to tomorrow or the next day. "Let's go lock up our classroom, and then we'll see about finding your mama for you, okay?" I run my hand over Jake's soft sandy-brown curls.

Needing a bit of space, I nudge Jake up and awkwardly push myself to standing. *Lord, I'm huge.*

Jake picks up the basket, empty now but for his gift bag and certificate, and carries it down the hall to our classroom. I still haven't decided whether I'm going to try and stay here, raising these babies on my own, or if I'm going home. Time is getting short, and I really need to make a decision soon, but my head and my heart are pulling me in two very different directions. I love it here, but twins might just be too much for me to handle without another set of hands.

I take the basket from Jake, handing him his gift bag. I'll keep hold of his certificate, so it doesn't go the way of the fake ones we handed them during the ceremony. Those were smashed to nothing, and you only graduate from kindergarten once. Best to have a little something to remember the day.

"Hey, bud. You about ready to go home?" Jack's voice drifts through the doorway, startling me.

"Where's my mom?" Jake asks shakily.

"She wasn't feeling well, so I took her home real quick. You want me to carry anything for you?" Jack asks both of us, I think.

Jack scoops Jake into his arms after the little guy mumbles, "Me," lifting his hands.

Sleepy Jake might just be my new favorite version of this kid because the way he's curled into Jack—head resting on broad shoulder, arms tucked up between them —melts my heart.

Moisture gathers in my eyes, and I curse the stupid hormones wreaking havoc with my emotions. I sling my bag over my shoulder, grab my keys and the rest of my stuff, and follow Jack out into the hall, locking the door behind us. We silently walk out of the building, and Jack clicks the locks on a small SUV, tucking Jake into the booster seat in the back.

"There you go," he says, snapping the seat belt into place. He shuts the door and turns to me, running a hand down his face. He looks exhausted, almost defeated.

I shift my bag to the other arm and hoist my free hand under my belly to support the weight, hoping for some relief to my back. "What happened?" I ask softly.

Jack presses his lips into a tight line, the muscles of his jaw jumping as he clenches and releases it. "I have to get Jake home. It's ... it's not good. Thank you for your help," he says stiffly. He drops his eyes to my stomach and shakes his head, mumbling, "Fucking hell," as he pulls open the car door and climbs in.

Fucking hell is right. I walk the short distance to my car —it's more of a waddle really—but since the principal gave me her parking spot for the last couple of weeks of school, I don't have far to go. When I've wedged myself behind the steering wheel, I look up and meet Jack's shadowed gaze. I'm glad he came tonight. I know it means the world to Jake, and with whatever went down with Chloe, it's good he's here to help. He nods once and pulls out of the lot but pauses before making it all the way to the intersection. My brain cells are dropping like flies, and I can't even begin to guess what he's doing. Instead, I start my car, turning in the opposite direction to head home.

This time last year, I was celebrating the end of another successful school year, slamming shots of Patrón at McBride's with my friends. Now, I can't wait to drop some cucumber slices in a big glass of water and crawl into bed. How times have changed, y'all.

As I turn the corner, I check my rearview mirror, and

Jack's taillights are gone. It would be so like him to wait and make sure that I was safely on my way before taking off himself.

I SLEEP FITFULLY, EVEN for me at this stage, constantly waking, wondering about what happened with Chloe Triplett last night. The text I sent Jack late last night, asking what had happened, remains unanswered. Nothing. So, when my phone rings as I'm pulling up to the school, I grab it and answer without even looking to see who's calling.

"Hey, how're my grandbabies this fine mornin'?" my mother's voice trills over the miles.

"Mornin', Mama," I answer, trying to stuff down my disappointment. "They're good, just wrestling before breakfast." Car parked, I grunt, pushing and shoving my way out of my Kia. It's not as easy as it used to be.

"You haven't eaten yet? Katelyn, go get you some breakfast. Those babies need calories, darlin' ..."

She carries on as I schlep myself across the drive and tap my ID card to the reader, gaining access to the school. I hightail it to the restroom because these two kiddos are not just wrestling; they're full-on tap-dancing on my bladder now.

"Mama, I have breakfast in my bag, but I've got to go. And, as much as I love you, I'm not chatting in the restroom. I'll call you later. Bye."

Lord have mercy, I'm not going to make it three more

months. Really, a little bit less than that, but still, it seems impossible.

I finish up and wave to Jenny as I pass the front office, determined to clean up my classroom—not just for the summer, but also in case I decide not to come back. If Mama would just come up and help me for a couple of weeks—maybe a month—I'm sure I could get us on a schedule and make my life up here work. It'd be hard, but I know I could do it. Maybe.

But, with my sister-in-law delivering about the same time, I know—I just *know*—it would kill Mama to have to choose. To miss out on time with one grandbaby in exchange for others. She'd feel like she was picking favorites.

I look around at the classroom I love, knowing in my heart that, unless some kind of miracle happens, I'm most likely kissing Beekman Hills good-bye.

The morning flies by with a million and one potty breaks, tons of boxes packed up, and more than a few tears shed. I really don't want to go back to Mississippi. Lord, the gossip over my return would about kill me.

Somehow, during the course of packing this particular box, my tape has rolled just out of reach. I need it. I'm starving, I have to pee again, and my damn tape is about three inches too far away. Why the hell did I think it was a good idea to sit on the floor to do this anyway? Right, because standing means bending over, and sitting in a chair is just not as practical.

I lean back against my pretty pink reading chair and close my eyes for just a minute's rest. One of the babies stretches, a small lump forming under my ribs. With two fingers, I push back, smiling as we start what I swear has become one of my favorite games. Push and shove. Hand-to-hand—or maybe foot—I play this little game, wondering which baby is my opponent in this round, guessing at the body part he's playing with.

"That's pretty amazing."

My eyes fly open to find Jack leaning in the doorway, a to-go bag from McBride's in his hand, the smell of something deep fried tickling my senses.

"It is," I agree. "Come on in and have a seat. I'd get up, but that could take a while." My heart skitters in my chest, not sure whether to beat harder or stop all together.

Jack showing up here today was about the last thing I expected, and Lord knows, there's no way of telling how this conversation'll go.

Jack walks into the room, filling the space somehow. The tan he had in the fall is deeper now, his skin a golden bronze. He plucks my water cup off my desk and then hands it to me, lowering himself to the floor.

"How're Chloe and Jake?" I ask, still only guessing about last night's events.

"Not good." He clears his throat and pulls black containers of chicken tenders and fries from the bag, setting them on the floor between us. "I took a chance that you'd be here getting shit organized today. Is this okay?" he asks.

"It's perfect, thank you." I pop the lid and snag a couple of fries, shoving them in my mouth. "Mmm, God, that's good," I practically moan.

"Yeah, I went to that Irish pub you used to talk about. I probably should have gotten something healthy for you, but this just sounded good. Comfort food, I guess." I'm fixing to ask who was working when he continues, "The girl behind the bar insisted on giving me extra tubs of ranch and hot sauce. She seemed pretty committed to the idea, so …"

"Yeah, that was Gracyn then. My old roommate," I say. "And this is exactly the way they should be eaten." I dip a chicken finger in the hot sauce and then dunk it in ranch, licking the extra sauce off my fingers. "So good."

27

Jack

I HAD A SNEAKING suspicion that the girl behind the bar was Kate's roommate, but former?

"She moved out?"

Kate nods while she chews. "Yeah, her boyfriend bought a house, and she moved right in," she says, dabbing at a dot of ranch that dribbled onto her belly.

Passing her a napkin, I say, "That was quick. Did she even know him when we were ..." When we were what? Dating, fucking? And fast? Jesus, Kate fucking jumped into bed with me while pregnant.

She snorts a laugh through her nose and shoves another bunch of fries in her mouth. She bobs her head from side to side. "Sorry, I didn't realize I was so hungry. Um, it seems quick, but they met more than two years ago, kind of lost touch, and then reconnected right before we met, so"—she shrugs and pushes at the side of her belly—"it's all good."

She wipes her hands and grabs another piece of chicken, mixing hot sauce into the ranch as she does her dipping thing. "Tell me what happened last night. I thought Jake's dad was going to be there."

I can't. It hasn't even really settled in yet, so I sure as shit can't say the words out loud. I shake my head and look at her—really look at her—not holding back or hiding where my focus is. "Tell me about this first. I think you should have told me you were pregnant when we were together. I kinda feel like that's not something you just hide." Maybe I'm being a little bit of a dick. "Christ, especially after the condom obliterated. You should have come clean about being with someone, unprotected, before. Do you have any idea of the risk you threw at me?" Totally being a dick.

"Wow. Okay, I guess we're doing this now," she says, dropping the chicken back in the box and laying both hands on her—what's bigger than a basketball? Because that bump is huge.

"And should you even still be working this far along? You look like you could drop that kid any minute." I should keep my mouth shut. Should bite my fucking tongue, but I've started it now, so I might as well finish. "And where the fuck is the father? He's okay with you working like this? Packing boxes and moving shit around? What kind of asshole is he?"

I don't lose my cool—ever—but the past eighteen hours have me so wound up that I can hardly see straight.

Kate's shock? I see that.

The hurt that clouds her expression? Can't miss it.

The flip to anger? That starts with a heated red flush at the top of her decidedly bigger tits and rises straight up her neck until I'm wondering if I just pissed her off enough to start labor.

"You tell me," she says, way too calm for anything good to be coming.

If I were a smarter man, I'd be catching on to what she just said, but no, I'm still stupid kinds of fired up.

"Why? Should I know him? That douche-bag doctor you were dating? Is that who it is?" I snort, honestly disgusted with my lack of control and rational thinking as much as the idea of that asshat knocking her up.

"You know him better than you think. But I'm blown away by how little you think of me." She struggles, shifting her legs so that one is out straight and the other is tucked in tight, her foot resting on the side of her thigh.

Kate pulls a deep breath into her lungs, blowing it out like the adjustment to her position took a lot out of her. *Why the hell is she still at work?*

She purses her lips, the dimple on her left cheek popping a little. "I'm due at the end of the summer." She runs one hand down the side of her stomach and then pushes gently, like she's repositioning the baby. "And the father doesn't entirely know," she says quietly.

"How does that work, Kate? You've either told him or you haven't. Which is it?"

She pins me in place and screws up her mouth again. Tilting her head to the side, she says, "I had no way of getting in contact with him—until now. And, yes, I look like a beached whale, like I'm ready to explode, because there are two babies in there."

Wait.

"They're yours, Jack. The condom ..." She shakes her head.

No.

"You sent me a text. Said you got your period, that we were clear," I throw back at her.

How the fuck did this happen?

"The doctor said that happens sometimes, that there's some spotting when they attach, nestle in there. I didn't lie, Jack. I didn't set out to do this on purpose, any of it. It happened. And you were gone."

Fuck my life.

"Two? Twins? Are you sure?" My brain is not firing on all cylinders because then I add my death knell, "You're sure they're mine?"

Kate stares at me like I'm stupid because I *abso-fucking-lutely* am.

"Yes, Jack. I'm fucking sure that there are two little aliens in there, dancing on my bladder, keeping me awake at night, wrestlin' and fightin' already like little boys do. Can I prove that they're yours? Sweet Jesus, not at this God-given moment. But there's no need to worry your pretty little head about it. You don't want to be a part of their lives? I won't make you. We'll be fine on our own. Made it this far without any help ..."

Wow. I mean, wow.

In less than a day, I went from a happy fucking bachelor—living my life, thinking about a repeat performance of the last time I had been here—to having not just one family to take care of, but two.

It took some time, but I finally pieced together the story from last night. Tripp had taken a knife to the chest. Totally a freak thing because I know—*I know*—the man can fight. I've seen him in a knife fight—trained with him, for fuck's sake—and if it wasn't for some stupid fucking luck, Tripp would've had the two guys subdued or in body bags without breaking a sweat. But some punk got the jump on him. I can *guaran-damn-tee,* though that, in his final seconds, when he realized he was done, Tripp fought his ass off and did some serious damage to the kid.

Doesn't matter that it was in a gas station just across the New York–New Jersey state line and not in the desert. He died, looking out for someone who couldn't help themselves. He died, protecting someone who needed it. Tripp died a hero.

And the calls? Tripp had me listed in his phone as his emergency contact. Thought shit news to Chloe would be better coming from me than a stranger. So, that stream of calls I ignored last night was nothing more than me failing in my duty to my brother. I fucking let him down, and now, I have to pay for that. Step up and take care of Chloe and Jake.

This, with Kate? I don't know. I just don't fucking know. I need a bottle of añejo tequila. I need some time to think. I need to process some serious shit and wrap my head around this mess.

She's sitting as still as can be, the picture of absolute

calm in the storm of my emotions. Waiting to see what she's going to get from me. And I'm not proud of what I give her, not in the least.

No, I stand up, easy as you please because the only body I have to move is my own. And I walk to the door of Kate's classroom. When I get there, I pause because she asked me a question, and I owe her an answer. And, while the answer to that particular question should be given with some kind of compassion, that's not something I can find in my shattered heart. It's out of reach along with my rapidly retreating sanity.

Since I have nothing left today, compassion or sanity, I turn and take in every last detail of Kate. The tendrils of hair escaping her messy bun. The dark smudges of exhaustion under her eyes. The stain from the ranch she dripped on the rolling waves of her stomach. Her hands splayed across her belly, our babies safely nestled in there.

And then I tell her, "Tripp's dead. He was stabbed in a gas station when he stopped to grab a cup of coffee on his way home from the airport."

And then I walk away.

Kate

I KNEW JAKE HAD lost his daddy, that Chloe Triplett had lost her husband. Deep down in my heart, I knew, but it was the last thing I wanted to deal with. And how selfish is that? Chloe and Jake don't get to choose whether they want to face it or not. They're stuck with it for the rest of their lives.

Rocking from side to side, I get my hands up on the seat of my reading chair and wedge my feet as close to my butt as I can get them. With a deep-ish, bracing breath, I hoist myself off the floor and slide into the chair. Not my most graceful moment, but I'm up. Mostly. And, now, I need to move. I can't sit here any longer today—not because of the babies, but because people are hurting. People who mean a lot to me.

Tears gather in my eyes, and I brush them away, taking in the mess around me. I clean up the food and trash, sling my bag over my shoulder, and head out. My pace is already slow, but I take it down another notch, praying I don't see Jack as I go. I'm not sure I can go another round with him.

"You okay, doll?" Jenny asks as I pass through the office, checking my mail.

"You heard about Jake's dad?"

She smiles a sad smile. "I did. When I went out last night, I caught a bit of it. That poor, precious boy."

I nod because the tears are making another appearance. I just can't imagine what Chloe is going through, her family broken, her hopes dashed. Maybe it's better for Jack to not be a part of our lives. I don't know if I could handle having that love, that partnership, and then have it ripped away. Maybe it's better to just do this thing on my own.

Jenny hands me a tissue. "Life is messy, Kate. But missing out on the good things because you're afraid of what might happen is no way to go through it. Sometimes, you have to jump, have faith, and put your heart on the line. The risk can be scary, but oh, the reward." She gives my hand a couple of quick squeezes. "Go on, sweetie. Get on out of here."

She's right. In fact, her simple words of wisdom sound a lot like the little speech I gave Gracyn when she was struggling over what to do about her relationship with Gavin. Lord, it is so much easier to see the trees in someone else's forest than it is when it's in your own backyard.

I whisper a, "Thank you," and give Jenny an awkward hug before going.

She's been mothering me since I started teaching here, almost like she knew I needed a soft place every now and again.

If I go, I'm going to miss her something fierce.

28

Kate

"**Y**OU READY, HOT MAMA?" Gracyn calls as she pushes through my apartment door.

The hot part is right. Even for the end of June, it feels beastly hot out.

"Just about." *Nope. Not in the least.* How ready can you ever be for a funeral, let alone one for a young father and husband? "Be honest, Gracyn. How bad do I look?"

I've been living in stretchy pants for months, my options dwindling every day, and even the biggest of my maternity clothes are stretched to their limits at this point. I'm desperately afraid of a wardrobe malfunction at any given time these days.

"Um, you look fine." Gracyn doesn't sound all that sure. "Is that the dress you just got last month?" She leans back, her eyes assessing the black ruched monstrosity.

"Yep. It's bad, isn't it?" I pull at the gathered fabric stretched around my massive bump.

She shakes her head and smiles. "No, but damn, you're—"

"Don't," I warn, cutting her off before she says something that I'll have to hate her for.

"It's just—"

"Gracyn, please stop," I plead. "I'm about as uncomfortable as I can be. It's hot out, and this whole thing is gonna suck bad, so just lie to me. Tell me I look pretty, and let's go."

Because she's one of my very best friends, she does just that. "You look gorgeous, Kate. Absolutely perfect. Come on. Lis is out front, waiting on us." She carries my tote bag for me, running ahead to push the elevator button. "You have your water bottle in here? Tissues?"

"Mmhmm. Not much point in bringing it unless it's stuffed full of all the shit we could possibly ever need," I say, huffing and puffing to catch up to her. *When did the elevator get so far from my front door?*

Hot, humid air about knocks the breath from me when we step outside of my building. This used to be my favorite time of year, but now, it's just miserable.

Grateful that Lis has the air-conditioning pumping, I wedge myself into her front passenger seat, muttering, "Fucking hell."

Lis reaches a hand over, smoothing my seat belt where it twisted as I clicked it. "Kate, I'm so sorry. I know what Jake means to you, and to lose his father so soon, it breaks my heart. Is there anything we can do for him and his mom?"

Blinking rapidly, I shift my gaze to the ceiling of her car and try to will my tears away. "I don't know. I can't even begin to imagine where to start, what to do."

Gracyn settles her hand on my shoulder and asks, "How did she sound when you talked to her?"

"I didn't. I, uh … Jack told me about the accident, and I Googled to find the funeral arrangements." I sigh, leaning my head against the headrest.

"Jack? You didn't tell us he was here. How did that go? Is he …" Gracyn stops mid-question, searching for the right words.

I slide my seat belt in my hand, holding it away from my body. "He showed up at graduation. Thank God he was there to take care of Chloe and get her settled before coming back for Jake. But seeing him like this was beyond awkward." I shift in my seat, glancing over my shoulder to look at Gracyn. "And he brought me lunch the next day from McBride's. You met him, G."

"Holy shit. Tall? Dark hair? A body you could climb? That was him?" She's far too excited for where this shit-show is going to end up.

"Mmhmm. Brought me my favorite lunch and—"

"And you told him about the babies. I mean, obviously, he could see, but you *told* him that they're his. How'd that go?" Lis prods.

I don't know whether to laugh or cry, so I manage both. "He asked me if I was sure they were his."

"No," Lis gasps.

"And he stormed out of my classroom after telling me that Mr. Triplett was dead. So, I'm thinking it's a pretty safe bet that he wasn't too excited to hear the news." I shrug, batting at the tears rolling down my cheeks.

Just because the logical part of me had expected that exact reaction from him doesn't mean there wasn't hope for a fairy-tale ending.

THE SERVICE IS AWFUL in the way that all funerals are.

Jake and his mama softly sobbing in the very front, closest to the casket holding their daddy and husband. Jack next to them, his posture braced and rigid. Parents, siblings, aunts, and uncles are all around them. Men in uniform dot the pews.

To the side of the flag-draped coffin sits a pair of combat boots with a rifle standing upright, a helmet and dog tags completing the battlefield cross. Chills run across my shoulders and down my spine. This is so much worse than I anticipated.

A hush falls over the chapel, and the national anthem plays. The chaplain gives the invocation, and then Jack stands, making his way to the podium, face pale. Jaw tight. The freewheeling and fun man I met in the fall is gone, replaced with one I hardly recognize. Detached, stoic, and somber, his expression unreadable.

"On behalf of the Triplett and Franks families, I would like to thank you all for attending," he begins.

"Today ..." Jack's voice succumbs to the finality of this moment, catching as he chokes down his emotions. He clears his throat, bracing his hands on the podium, taking a beat to compose himself. "We've gathered today to say farewell to Sergeant Dallas Henry Triplett, father, husband, son, brother, and friend. The world is a lesser place without him.

"George S. Patton is quoted as saying, 'It is foolish and wrong to mourn the men who have died. Rather we should thank God that such men existed.' I thank God that I had Tripp in my life. To have been included in his. To have served with him, learned with him, laughed with him, and cried with him. He was my best friend, my brother in arms. The man I entrusted with my life."

Hot tears blur my vision, silently cascading down my cheeks. As Jack speaks about Tripp, my heart crumbles. Chloe's head drops forward, her shoulders shaking with grief.

The future they planned together, their entire life, is gone. Their course forever changed. Jake will be the only child Tripp and Chloe have, and that little boy is clinging to his grandpa, his body wrung out from tears.

Jack talks about Tripp's accomplishments in the service and how they met. The things he learned from Tripp and what he admired most. The way Tripp was able to set aside the hardships and demands of his job, a job that he loved and believed in, and be the very best father and husband when he was at home. How he seemed to flip a switch, not contaminating the sanctity of his family with the ugliness of war.

"Finally, an unknown author wrote, *The brave may not live forever, but the cautious do not live at all.* Tripp lived every day to its fullest." Jack pauses, looking toward his best friend's casket. "And he was the bravest man I knew."

The scripture is read; the hymn is played. A moment of silence is offered, but the room echoes with the sound of sniffles and sobs. Death sucks, but a senseless loss like this is so, so much worse. The boys who killed Tripp stole his rental car and crashed it after a joy ride. They got fifty dollars in cash from the register and a ride in the back of a police car. So damn stupid.

After the chaplain delivers the benediction, I breathe a little sigh of relief.

"The service will continue at Beekman Hills Memorial Cemetery. We ask that you join us, if you're able, to pay your final respects there." He nods, and with crisp precision, six of the men in blue uniforms carry the flag-draped casket up the center aisle.

Jack escorts Chloe, her arm through his, his hand wrapped around hers. His eyes staring straight ahead.

My tears start up all over again, watching the show that not one of us wants to attend.

"Kate, you okay?" Lis asks softly, her hand gently rubbing my shoulder.

"I'm good," I whisper.

Because, if nothing else, a funeral puts everything back in perspective, acts as a reminder not to get caught up in the little things but to look deep within, holding close the things that are important and casting off the rest among the tombstones.

The pews empty, faces downcast, tissues dabbing at bloodshot eyes. Gracyn steps out into the aisle and reaches out for my hand. Feeling more than a little off-balance, I take her hand and maneuver my bulk out of the pew. My best friends walk with me, out of the cool chapel and into the blazing heat. How can the sun deign to shine at a time like this?

The graveside service is what does me in though. A handful of chairs set up on the side of the hill. The plot is shaded, thank God, a light breeze stirring the leaves of the trees overhead.

We're not far from where Francie is buried, and Gracyn and Lis each glance in the direction of his grave.

"Y'all can go visit him," I say softly. "I'll be fine right here."

"I'm good," Gracyn says, squeezing my hand.

Lis adds, "I just came by yesterday."

I hit the jackpot when I stumbled on these two. They walk with me, our progress slow, up the slight incline to the sun-dappled gravesite.

A hush falls over the gathering as the hearse doors are opened. Chloe and Jack walk quietly behind the casket, her hand periodically reaching out. Reaching for her husband, not ready to let him go. The family settles in the chairs—Chloe and Jake, her parents and Tripp's. His sister and Chloe's brothers. Tripp's granddad, bless him, offers me his chair. Him leaning on his cane, me with this belly.

"Thank you, sir, but I'm just fine," I whisper.

I can't take his chair. I just can't stand the idea of getting any closer, like this whole thing is contagious and I could somehow be next if I got too close.

After the chaplain says a few words, all the

uniformed service members shift, standing tall, hands held in loose fists that are precisely lined up with the yellow stripes down their legs. One of them, his uniform slightly different from Jack's, moves to stand next to the casket.

"Staff Sergeant Riojas," he calls in a booming voice.

"Here, Team Sergeant," comes the response.

"Sergeant First Class Baker."

"Here, Team Sergeant."

"Sergeant Vance."

"Here, Team Sergeant."

"Sergeant Triplett."

Silence. Of course, because Tripp is dead.

"Sergeant Dallas Triplett."

Why is he doing this? It's cruel.

"Sergeant Dallas H. Triplett."

The only sound is a gasped sob from Chloe as she pitches forward in her folding chair, her hand shaking over her mouth. Jack wraps an arm around her shoulders, pulling her to him. Supporting her because without him holding her up, holding her back, she looks like she could throw herself across her husband's casket.

I sway forward with her as she tries again to reach for Tripp.

Lis grabs me, pulling me back to balance. "Gracyn, get her water bottle," she hisses. "Kate, take a drink."

"I'm fine," I insist. I'm fine. I'm okay. This is not about me.

Gracyn shoves my water bottle into my hand anyway, lifting it toward my mouth. I don't have the energy to fight about this right now, so I take a sip, only to drop the bottle to the ground at the sound of rifle fire.

The retort echoes across the hill again.

And once more as Chloe weeps.

Jake startles, crying out, "My daddy. I want my daddy."

Lis and Gracyn move quickly as my knees buckle slightly, and I reach for the large maple tree behind me. As heartbreaking as Francie's funeral was this spring, this one is so much worse. So much.

The chilling strains of "Taps" rise up, sunlight glinting off the bugle.

"Kate, let's get you to the car," Gracyn says.

I shake my head, unwilling to try to form words.

"It's okay. We'll just—"

"No," I croak out. "Not yet." I cling to my friends as the flag is removed from the casket, folded precisely, smoothed, and presented to Chloe with three brass shell casings resting on top.

With a heavy heart, I nod finally. The flag clutched to Chloe's chest, Jake sobbing, and Jack tending to them is enough for me.

My heart breaks as I turn away, whispering, "Take me home."

29

Jack

I WATCH THROUGH A haze of grief as Kate and her friends arrive at the memorial. My eyes drawn to her at every opportunity. Her teary gaze dragging from the casket of my fucking hero to the wife and child he left behind while I delivered the eulogy.

Useless fucking words—that's all they were. There's no way to capture the things that made Tripp the man he was or even come close to doing him justice.

Tripp entrusted me with taking care of his family when he was no longer able. It's the kind of conversation you have when you've waded through hell and made it back out the other side. A promise made that never in your wildest dreams do you think you'll have to fulfill because the person you make that vow to is nothing short of invincible.

That was Tripp—invincible until he wasn't.

Every gasp that Chloe made, every sob from Jake wrenched at my heart. My focus needs to be one hundred percent on Tripp's family.

So, I brace as rigidly as I can, practically holding Chloe up as she follows her husband down the aisle of the chapel. Eyes forward, hand covering hers where her fingers dig into my arm, guiding her down this hellish gauntlet to the car that will ferry us to a final good-bye.

Compartmentalization is my saving grace. I've had so much thrown at me in such a short amount of time; it's the only way I'm able to keep my shit together.

Give me a mission and an objective, and I'm fine. I can analyze the fuck out of what needs to happen—communications, transportation, the desired outcome—and choreograph the steps it takes to see it through. It's ingrained in me. Pounded into me by the very best of the best—my team, my friends, my brothers.

I've trained for that. I can dissect the situation, find our marks, and make shit happen.

Burying Tripp was never part of that mission.

And, now, there's Kate. Every shift, every sway of her body pulls at me, making me want to go to her. Wrap her in my arms and make up for everything I missed, and at the same time, I want to run fucking far and fast.

The news that she's pregnant hasn't even settled in yet, and twins ... twins are a fucking shock. But there is no denying that the belly she's got is home to some crazy, active boys. My active boys. Jesus Christ, this is not what I planned, not for an instant.

A million times, it's run through my head that Tripp

had a gift for making this shit work, the job and a family. Most of the guys do and do it well. I don't think I have that skill, and I've never fucking wanted it. Maybe that's the missing piece. Maybe that's my failure.

Kate's retreating form is surrounded and supported by her friends, each holding tight to her. Guiding her down the hill to a small sedan. When she is tucked into the passenger seat, I squint into the blazing sun, looking for the shift of her body, the glint of metal showing that she's buckled in safely.

"Go. You need to talk to her." Chloe's voice is hoarse, thick with all the tears she's shed and the ones still to come.

"I'm good."

"I know. You're fine. You know the definition of fine, right?"

Everyone knows the stupid definition. "Freaked out. Insecure. Neurotic. And Emotional. Yeah, but you and Jake are my priority. Tripp—"

"He'd want you to go take care of *your* family," Chloe rasps, her breath catching on her words. "You know he would, Jack. I know you didn't plan for any of this to happen, but Ms. Beard is the nicest, sweetest ... well, I'm guessing you actually know all of that already. Otherwise, there wouldn't be two sweet baby boys getting ready to join the world. You know your heart, Jack. And, however you feel about balancing a family with your career, that doesn't change the fact that you have a family now. Babies, Jack. Boys who need their father—for whatever time God sees fit to give you with each other.

"My parents are here, Tripp's parents. Jake and I are covered, really. And, God, all I want to do is go home and crawl into bed. I want to close my eyes and pretend for just one more day that he's going to be there when I wake up. That Jake'll have just one more day with his dad."

My molars grind against each other; the muscles in my jaw clench and tighten. It actually feels like every muscle in my body is contracted, locked down, and ready to explode. "I know. I will. I'll take care of things. But I need to see things through with this. Get you and Jake settled, make sure you're squared away."

"Okay," Chloe concedes. "But then I'm kicking your ass out, Jack."

Shaking my head, I allow the corners of my mouth to lift into the briefest of smiles because, damn, after all the time they've been married, Tripp is alive in Chloe. "You sound just like him."

TRUE TO HER WORD, Chloe granted me the honor of escorting her and her family home. Seeing that they had everything they needed.

And then she pushed me out the door. "You promised. Just go take care of your own business."

On the way back to my hotel—the same damn one down to the motherfucking room that I stayed in last time I was here—I stop by the Irish pub. Honestly, I'm shocked to see the blonde chick who was with Kate earlier behind the bar. The redhead sitting across from her turns to face me, my beret clasped between my hands.

"Is Kate ... *shit*."

The looks from these two are enough to stop me in my tracks. I don't know why I thought for even a minute that Kate wouldn't have told her best friends about how I handled the news.

"Sorry. I'm Jack. We've not had the pleasure of meeting yet." I offer my hand, fully expecting to be blown off.

The blonde glares, scrubbing at the pristine bartop in front of her. "Because you were too busy fucking our friend last time you were in port," she spits the words like daggers.

"For the love of God, Gracyn, you don't have to be such an ass." The redhead shakes my hand, offering, "I'm Lis. It's good to meet you."

"Is it though? Really?" the blonde mutters.

"And this is Gracyn, but she seems to be struggling with manners today." Lis pops a side-eye at Gracyn, the former roommate.

And then, with a blink and a sigh, her demeanor changes, throwing me into a different kind of discomfort. "I'm so sorry for your loss. How's his family doing? Kate loves that little boy."

Emotions reach up, clawing at my throat, and I have to swallow them down to speak. "Thank you. They're doing as well as can be expected. Family is with them right now, and the team"—I clear my throat because the team will never be the same without Tripp—"will look out for Chloe and Jake."

"And you?" Gracyn asks.

"They're family. That won't ever change."

"What about your other family? What about your responsibilities to Kate and those babies? What about them?" She pulls a bottle of Patrón from the top shelf behind the bar and pours herself a healthy glass, two fingers easy. Maybe three.

Sliding a twenty across the bar, I nod at the tequila, and after a contemplative sip, she concedes, pouring a splash for me and then topping off her own.

"I appreciate your concern"—I lift my glass to this fierce friend—"but I believe that's between Kate and me." I swallow a paltry amount of tequila and set the glass back on the bar. "Is she at home?"

Lis doesn't have half the attitude that Gracyn is sporting and nods. "She is. Today took a lot out of her, I think."

"Thank you. Is there anything you can think of that she needs? I'm happy to stop on the way."

Silently, Lis shakes her head. And, with a final nod, I turn, the crisp click of my dress shoes matching the beat of my heart as I cross to the door.

"Why'd you come here first?" Gracyn's question pulls me to a stop.

I wondered which one of the women would ask, if they would ask.

"Because you're important to Kate. You've been here for her while I wasn't, and I owe you an introduction and my heartfelt thanks." Pushing out the door, I put my beret on, arranging the flash above my left eye, and hope that answer was enough.

. . .

THREE SHARP RAPS ON her door get me nothing. Three more and a small bit of patience get me some slow shuffling and a call to hang on. When the door finally opens, something deep in my chest cracks wide open. Gone is the black dress from earlier in the day, the swaths of fabric that wrapped her up, accentuating her curves. Now, a T-shirt I haven't seen since our weekend in the mountains strains across her belly and pale gray pajama pants end just below her knees. Eyes puffy with tears.

And she has never looked more beautiful.

"What do you want, Jack?" Kate shifts her weight, one hand supporting our boys, the other pushing at her lower back. Light from the late afternoon sun glows through her hair. Beautiful. She shifts again and huffs a lock of hair out of her face.

"I came to apologize. Talk to you and figure this out, I guess. Can I come in?"

Beautiful, yes, but the way she's shifting her weight and pushing at her back, she's got to be massively uncomfortable.

Kate steps back into her apartment, waves toward the couch, and continues down the hall. "Make yourself comfortable. I'll be right back."

When she lowers herself down onto the gray velvet cushions several minutes later, she says, "Sorry, one of them was tap-dancin' on my bladder. And I should have offered you somethin' to drink before I sat down."

"Stop," I say, holding my hand out at her. "Let me. What do you need?"

"Water would be great. Help yourself to whatever you

want. I think there's a beer in the fridge—maybe. The good stuff is in the cabinet above."

I sift through the cabinets, finding what I need and, sweet mother of God, there's a half-full bottle of Casamigos Blanco in her liquor cabinet. I grab the bottle, tucking it under my arm, while balancing Kate's water and a glass of ice in my hand.

"You mind if I grab the bag of chips?"

"Have at it. Salsa's in the fridge."

I settle everything on the coffee table, handing Kate her water and splashing tequila into my glass. "Mind if I take off my jacket? I've, uh ... it'd be nice to relax a little." I push the polished brass buttons through, releasing the form-fitting jacket.

She waves her hand at me, tearing into the bag of tortilla chips instead. "*Oh-ma-Gawd*," she moans around a mouthful of chips.

I missed that moan. Although last time I heard it was under much different circumstances. The first time I'd heard it was evidently what got us here.

Kate rocks, pushing herself forward, reaching for the salsa.

"Here." I pop the top and hand the jar to her. "Do you need something more? Have you eaten today?"

"Jack, I eat constantly. All the time. These boys are already wreaking havoc." Kate snorts, dripping salsa on her shirt. My shirt. "Damn it. Every single time." She swipes at the dab of tomato resting on the swell of her breast. "So, what did you want to say? Thought you were crystal clear when you stormed out of my classroom, and that's fine. Really."

"It's not. Jesus, Kate, I was surprised. This past week—losing Tripp, finding out about this." I nod at her.

A corner of a chip tumbles from her lips, coming to rest on top of her belly. The chip moves, lifting and then settling again. Moved by what? One of our kids?

"Why didn't you contact me? Tell me you were—"

"How would you have had me do that? Send a text that you'd get at some point when you landed? Last text I sent was that we were in the clear, and you hardly responded to that. Thought you'd have been all kinds of receptive, gettin' an *oops, guess I was wrong 'bout that* text. Or should I have gone to my student's mother and asked her to let you know I was knocked up? That woulda been real professional. And did they, either of them, even know we were—"

"Tripp figured it out. That we were seeing each other, but he never said anything about ..." I wave at the big bump between us, a lump pushing out at an odd angle. "What is that?" I ask.

Kate reaches for my hand, placing it over the hard alien lump. Pushing against it. "A butt probably. Maybe a head. I don't really know."

The baby rolls, shifting away from the pressure, shoving his brother, so a different ass or body part rolls down the other side of Kate's belly.

"This happen all the time?" I ask, enthralled by the wrestling match taking place.

Laughing, Kate nods. "All the damn time. You have no idea. If they're not fighting each other, they're beating on me." She splays her hands, running them in lazy circles over her abdomen, humming softly, and her belly—our babies seem to relax before my eyes.

"Jesus, you're amazing." The words leave me on a reverent hush.

30

Kate

THE JACK SITTING IN my apartment is not the same
one who walked out of my classroom days ago. The
one who spit condescension and judgment at me as he
stonily walked away. This one is much more like the Jack I
spent a month wrapped up in, falling for.

"You're right; it would have been awkward, putting
Chloe in the middle of things. I just wish I had known." He
runs his hand down his face, his scruffy beard no longer
there.

He looks so different with his face smooth, hair
cropped short, and in that uniform. Even half-undone, his
jacket and tie neatly folded over the back of a chair, his
bearing is entirely something else. Familiar and, at the
same time, new.

"I wrote to you," I softly tell him. "Made sure to tell you

every little thing—doctor's appointments, when I first felt them move. All of it. God, I have pictures from the sonograms. Let me—"

"Stop, Kate." He stops my struggle to stand once again. "You need something, just tell me where it is. I'm here now."

He pushes himself off the couch with so much grace and ease, not like the lumbering whale I've become, having to roll to the side and heave myself up. There is nothing graceful or attractive about that. Nothing at all.

"I have to get up anyway."

But, instead of having to struggle up on my own, Jack is there. A strong hand, a firm grip. Someone to steady me as I make it to my feet. I hurry down the hall as fast as I can manage. I grab my journal, not sure that I can make it back to the living room with it before I have to pee, but Jack's right there. Silently filling my room.

"Here, I have to pee." I push past him to the bathroom, thrusting the journal into his hands, careful not to let the pictures flutter out.

"Not sure whether to laugh or—"

"Probably not the best idea right now. No one likes the guy who makes fun of the fat kid," I call through the door.

Instead of an empty room, I walk out of the bathroom to find Jack propped up against my headboard, sifting through grainy black-and-white pictures, his jaw working tightly. Fingers dancing over the images of our babies. Watching him process in mere moments all that I've had months to wrap my head around is sobering. I have no idea what those months of his life held. The things he did, the decisions he had to make, the lives he saw come and go.

But I do know what he came home to.

Jack tilts his head, his eyes drifting from the pictures clutched in his hand, the most recent ones, showing our babies' profiles, to where they're pushing on each other, fighting for space inside me. "They're really real, aren't they?" His gaze meets mine, eyes wide.

"Yeah." I chuckle. "There's no pretending going on here. Contrary to popular opinion, I did not go on a binge and just get super huge for kicks."

He jerks his head, looking totally offended. "Who said that?"

I pull my salsa-stained T-shirt over my head, my camisole underneath hiding next to nothing. "No one. Just feels that way sometimes. Not as much now. I mean, I'm for sure knocked up, but … I don't know."

He leans forward, scanning me from head to toe, eyes lingering on my boobs, my belly. Just as he opens his mouth to say something overly nice, I'm sure, his phone chirps with an incoming call. Checking the screen, he nods briefly. "I have to take this. I'm sorry."

"It's all good. Stay here. I'll go pee. Again."

Jack finishes his phone call, his voice the only indication that he's moving through my apartment. "Are you okay?" he asks, stepping into the kitchen, his warm hand heavy on my back.

"Lower. Put your hand lower on my back. God, yes,

right there." I manage to barely suppress a moan at the relief his hand gives me as I sway my hips from side to side, elbows resting on the kitchen island.

Jack makes a strangled noise deep in his throat.

"Sorry. I'm sure this is a sight, but there're times when leaning on the counter like this is the only thing that feels good. It's like all the pressure is off my organs for a hot minute."

I straighten my legs and push back, looking to deepen the stretch in my hips, but what I find is Jack. His free hand shoots to my hip, fingers digging in, holding me against him. My body lights up at the feel of him hard behind me.

"You have any idea what you're doing to me?" he rasps, his hard cock trapped between us.

He leans over me, chest to my back, and presses his lips to the back of my neck. It tingles down my spine. I push back into him again, rubbing my ass against his length.

Maybe it's just the hormonal hornies, but pent-up desire ignites as his hands roam and caress. Sliding up my sides, over my belly. Cupping my swollen breasts. The way he touches me is reverent, like he's worshipping the changes in my body.

"Mercy," he huffs, lips trailing electric kisses along down my spine, hips grinding into me. "Tell me you want this, Kate. God, tell me this is okay."

"Please ..." I gasp, my mind clouded with the need to feel more. To connect with Jack, to feel him in me, around me. With me. "I don't know how ... logistics ..." I start nervously.

Teeth sink into my hip as Jack steps away, his belt clattering open. The hiss of his zipper.

His wallet hits the counter beside me, and he fumbles it open, searching for a condom but coming up empty. Kind of a moot point at this stage anyway, but maybe he's had opportunities that I haven't. Maybe this isn't a good idea.

"Fuck." His head falls, forehead on my back as he dips his hand down the front of my jammie pants. "I swear, Kate, I haven't been with anyone since you, but"—his finger strums my clit, circling maddeningly—"I can still take care of you."

Moaning as he thrusts one thick finger and then two into my pussy, I rock shamelessly against him. "Mmm-mmm. I need you, Jack. Please," I gasp. "Need you."

Shoving my PJs and panties to the floor, Jack frees his cock, and achingly slow, he fills me. Almost immediately, my legs start to tremble.

"God, yes," he grunts, thrusting gently, hitting *that spot*, the one that makes my eyes roll back and all my inner muscles clench.

Pleasure rolls through me, exploding in delicious waves. Jack stills, breathing hard, and pulls away, hissing as his hard cock leaves my still-pulsing vag.

"Why did you stop?" I stand and face him.

"I didn't want to hurt them." He makes a sad attempt at stuffing his dick away, pain and determination written across his face.

Using my toes, I fling my panties and PJs up into my hand and shove Jack out of the kitchen and toward the bedroom. "Nope. You're big, but that's not a thing. You're not poking anyone in the eye, not causing brain damage, none of that. If you changed your mind and don't want to do this"—I drop my gaze to his groin—"just say so. But we both know you're lying."

Lord, I hope he's lying. I can't say that, at this stage of pregnancy, I feel all that attractive, just bloated and huge, more like a sumo wrestler than anything. But Jack's caressing hands wandering over my body, feeling what I thought was his genuine excitement, made me feel sexy for the first time in months. The other moms in my prenatal yoga class all talk about how their husbands make them feel amazing and confident, sexy and beautiful. Today with Jack is the first time I've come close to feeling anything like that.

And I want more. Even if it's just for as long as he's here. Again.

But why would he want me like this? We're nothing more than two people who broke a condom. Spectacularly.

"Wait, why are you walking away from me?" Jack asks. "Are you crying? Did I hurt you?" He clutches my face between his palms, thumbs swiping at the tears under my eyes.

I shake my head, feeling overwhelmingly stupid. Hating that, once again, I can't seem to control my tears.

"Kate, talk to me."

"It's nothing. I'm fine."

Jack chuckles softly and kisses me slowly. Thoroughly, deeply. "Freaked out, insecure, neurotic, and emotional. That's what *fine* stands for. What're you thinking about?"

"This hasn't been easy for me. Everyone I know who's pregnant has support, all kinds of support. Gracyn and Lis have been tremendously helpful, but this is ... it's hard. The small hint just now of what it would be like to have a partner in this. To not be alone. To feel like I'm still a person, a woman, and not just a breeding factory. Because it's hard to feel attractive for a minute, let alone sexy. And I felt that out there."

I have lost my damn mind. I know it with every fiber of my being. Words are tumbling from my mouth, emotional vomit spewing across the room, thrown at the nearest target. "I shouldn't fuss. Thank you. That connection, however brief, is what I needed. Or maybe it was the orgasm that I needed, but really, I'll be okay, and you've been more than gracious. You don't need to feel pressured into doing that again or anything."

Jack sits on the edge of my bed, pulling me toward him. "Katelyn, I assure you, I was not being gracious. Not in the least. A little scared? Yep, absolutely, but that was not a pity fuck or whatever." He slides his hands under my camisole, exposing my burgeoning belly. "Take this off. Let me see you. Feel you. Worship you. How can you think you're not attractive?"

Before my cami hits the floor, Jack's face is in my tits, licking at where they overflow the cups of my bra. Swiping his tongue between them where they're smashed together. With the flick of his fingers, the clasps are unhooked, and my breasts spill free.

"Everything about you is ripe and gorgeous. And there is nothing sexier than seeing you filled up with our babies.

Makes me want to keep you like this forever," he murmurs, sucking a sensitive nipple into his mouth.

I arch into him, digging my fingers into his shoulders until he pulls away, letting my nipple fall from his mouth with a gentle bite.

Jack pops the buttons on his dress shirt until it's free enough to pull over his head. Triceps flexing as he tosses it to the floor. He shimmies back into the middle of the bed, toeing off his shoes, shedding his thin blue pants and boxer briefs. "Come here. If you're in control, I won't feel like I'm gonna hurt you. Or them. But, sweet cheeks, I promise you, there is nothing I want more than to feel you sink down onto my dick and run my hands over every single one of your curves."

He holds his hand out for me, helping me to climb onto the bed and straddle his hips.

Never before in my life have I felt this exposed, this self-conscious. I wrap one arm across my chest, the other slanting down, futilely trying to cover up as much of my mass as I can.

"Don't you hide from me." He takes my hands, gently placing them on my thighs. "We did this amazing, unintentional thing. Neither of us saw this coming, but, Jesus, I can't stop thinking about the fact that we did this." His big hands spread across my belly, sliding up over the top, turning to cup my full breasts before roaming back down again. "How can you think you are anything other than sexy as fuck?"

Slowly rocking his hips, Jack lifts me, guiding me until he slides into me, and then he lets me take control of how much, how deep. And those sexy, confident feelings all come flooding back to me. His teeth sinking into his lip. His eyes caressing me, hands everywhere at once. Curses and prayers mumbled along with words of beauty.

The only thing missing is love.

31

Jack

I'M NOT A FOOL. I don't honestly think I have a magic dick that makes everything shiny in the world, but the change in Kate after we ... well, the word *fucked* isn't right. *Made love* feels closer to the truth, but goddamn, just thinking it makes me feel like I need to turn in my man card. I've done enough self-reflection, enough psych evaluations, to know that—for me at least—actions speak louder than words.

But the change in Kate pulled hard at my heart. That shit about not being attractive? Fuck no. She is stunning. I meant what I said to her about keeping her pregnant. All it took was Chloe's verbal slap upside the head and the reality of loss to bring me clarity, to confirm that I can do this. That I want this. The idea of being suckered did not sit well with me. Not at all. But ironing out those details in my mind, skimming through the journal she's been keeping, and seeing them—our boys had a bigger impact on me than I ever thought possible. How the fuck can seeing grainy black-and-white pictures of tiny humans twist something so drastically inside me?

Kate fell asleep almost immediately after she came. Well, after cleaning up our mess and pissing yet again. She crawled right into bed, nestling into me, her ass tucked in tight. How she sleeps with these two heathens pushing and kicking is beyond me. I rub my thumb across a bump —an elbow, maybe a knee—and chuckle at the push back from within. I get why her students were all about giving the babies high fives.

"They won't stop," Kate mumbles into the pillow. "They've got to be the most active kids ever."

"Probably how they were made, all rambunctious and with gusto."

"Gusto? What the hell with that word? Who talks like that?" She rubs her belly and laughs softly. "You know when they didn't move?"

"When I was bopping them on the head. So, now, we know how to get them to sleep once they're evicted." The kisses I trail across her shoulders are brought up short when she tenses. "What?"

"You're talking like you're going to be here, in our lives." She shakes her head and hides her face in her hands. "Don't do that if this isn't what you really want. You were super clear on not wanting to be stuck, Jack."

"The last thing I feel is stuck. I thought about you constantly. Talked to Tripp a lot, picked his brain. Team

Sergeant has four kids, and they're good ones. Manners, smart. Not at all entitled, belligerent hellions."

It takes a lot of effort, but Kate rolls toward me, our babies tucked between us. "If that were all it took, Jake would've been proof enough that Army brats weren't necessarily brats. What about the other stuff? Your family, the girl who tried to keep you in Montana?" Her eyes are wide, her expression completely open, and all the Southern drawl this girl possesses is out for the world to hear.

"I saw Jess when I was home for Christmas, met her daughter, too. She's still manipulative. Asked me to spend time with her while I was there. Pretty sure her husband wouldn't have appreciated that too much. And my family ..." *What the hell do I say about them?* "My dad worked me hard, fixing fences and tending to the ranch. Told the town and the entire family that I was done playing soldier and was coming home to take over the ranch—do real work."

"Seriously? What would make him do that?"

"Purely selfish. He thinks I should be there, so that's all he can see. What he didn't expect were my twin sisters and their husbands taking exception to that."

"You have twin sisters? Really? You couldn't have mentioned that?"

"Yeah. Didn't exactly plan on all this." I trail my fingers down her side, tickling her as I get low on her bump.

"So, did they set your dad straight or what?"

"We all did. My brothers-in-law were ready to walk away. Ironically, they're brothers, not twins, but close enough—"

"Irish twins? That's what Francie used to call them, when he was still alive. Just nine months or so apart."

"That's about right. Who's Francie?" I ask.

"He owned the pub before." Kate sighs, looking like tears'll come any minute. "Before he passed away on St. Patrick's Day. He was an amazing man, a father when you needed one, a businessman who knew when to break the rules and how to take risks. He was the kindest, fiercest friend with a ready smile, a bad joke, and bit of wisdom. His only drawback was that he was a whiskey drinker and not a fan of tequila at all. But he did order a bottle of Patrón for the bar just for me."

I swipe at the tears gathering in her eyes. "I'm so sorry."

"He didn't want to bother any of us—Lis and Gracyn mostly and Finn—with the fact that he had cancer. So, he kept it hidden, put things in place so that the pub and the family he'd collected would all be taken care of. He was a good man. He's buried not far from Tripp." She takes a deep, cleansing breath, expelling sadness, painting a watery smile on her face. "Sorry. Tell me more about your brothers-in-law."

"Jesus, Kate, I'm so sorry. I would've liked to have met him and maybe ... I don't know ... shared a whiskey with him." I tuck a lock of hair behind her ear, the strand like silk between my fingers. Hating even more that she was hurting and I missed it, all of it. I huff out my frustration and continue, "Anyway, their grandfather died, left them some money and some land. Told my pops that, after all they'd done for him, for the ranch, that he'd best not push them aside for someone who didn't even want to be there.

The guys at least talk with me once in a while and know full well that I don't want that life. There is nothing but respect in both directions, but relations are strained, to say the least. Despite all of that, I was headed there post-deployment to help with calving, but Tripp made a better argument for coming back here instead, and thank God for that." I brush my lips across her forehead.

"WHEN DID THEY GO from Baby A and Baby B to M and D?" I shuffle through the pictures of the babies again as Kate brings a basket of baby clothes to the kitchen island. "And what's with *Oops* and *Uh-oh* in your journal?"

A deep, sexy laugh bubbles up out of Kate, shaking her tits, distracting me. "*Oops*—well, I think that's self-explanatory. And, once the doctor told me there were two, *Uh-oh* seemed the perfect fit until I could decide on names."

"We're coming back to the name thing in a minute, but why did you wait so long to go to the doctor?" I ask. Little by little, piece by piece, we've spent the past couple of weeks reliving the six months we were apart. Kate sharing the details of what she went through alone, and me trying to make up for not being here for her.

"I was scared to face reality. Wanted to hide from it for as long as I could. It was stupid, not a good choice, but I'm human. And I was alone."

I can't argue with her, not with the way I ran when she told me the boys were mine. "Fair enough. And the names? What did you decide?"

"Mason and Dixon Beard. Thus the switch on the

sonogram pics." She quirks her mouth and looks at me out of the corner of her eye. "Unless you have a really strong objection," she adds.

And do I fucking ever.

"Mason and Dixon are fine. I like the North-South thing you've got going on, but—"

"It's less to do with that than you think. My great-granddaddy was a mason—a bricklayer really. And I thought you'd told me you grew up near Dixon. Is that right? I thought I'd honor both of our families in some way." She smiles and rolls her eyes before adding, "And these two are probably the only reason my mama crossed the Mason-Dixon Line at all, so—"

Mesmerized, I watch as Kate folds tiny little T-shirts with the snap things at the bottom, each one ending up in a precise rectangle. She'd make any drill sergeant proud.

"I like it. Mind if I make a suggestion though?"

She tosses me a shirt to fold and leans over the counter, ass out, back flat, braced on her forearms. She's told me it feels good, relieving pressure, but I'll be damned if I have any kind of capacity to think when she does that. She sways her ass from side to side and eyes me like she's waiting on me to speak.

"Right." I clear my throat. "Mason Triplett *Jackson* and Dixon—"

"Dixon Wyatt Jackson?" she asks.

I hate that I share a name with my asshole father, but maybe between the two of us, Dixon and I—and Jake—can do the name proud.

Adding my rectangle of baby undershirt to the pile, I smirk. "I like that. Just one more thing we need to change."

I reach for the box I'd tucked away in the back of the liquor cabinet last week, just waiting for the right moment. I knew the night of Tripp's funeral, when she let me in, that this day was on the horizon, I just needed to get things in place for it.

"Are you going to show off, drinking the good tequila in front of me again? Makes you more of an ass than the sweet man you know you should be around a ridiculously pregnant woman," she says snarkily. "Think you'd know better by now. Is there even going to be any of that left by the time I can drink it? I swear to God, you're doing this just to get under my skin." With her forehead resting on her folded arms, Kate's voice echoes hollowly against the countertop. She's officially hit the miserable stage from what her doctor said at last week's appointment.

The black box makes a quiet *shoosh* as I slide it across the granite counter until it rests right in front of her arms. "What's this?" she asks, plucking at the gray and gold bow. Finally, the ribbon falls free, and Kate lifts the tight-fitting lid to reveal two pint-sized black hoodies with the USMA cadet crest emblazoned on the fronts—one in gray, the other in gold.

"Oh, Jack, they're adorable," Kate exclaims, pulling the sweatshirts out one at a time and holding them up for inspection. "Shit, I think they left the sensor on this one." She reaches her fingers into the pocket on the front of the hoodie, practically turning it inside out to get to what is most definitely *not* a store-theft sensor.

"Oh my God." Kate slowly lifts her head, her gaze meeting mine.

I take the diamond ring from her trembling fingers, clasping her left hand in mine. "Kate, somehow, someway, you've done what no one has ever been able to do. From your disastrous history of dating pencil-dicked douche bags to the scariest busted condom removal ever. From one month of a good time to six months of stress and worry. From tombstones to bassinets, you've shown me that we can not just survive in the face of strife, but also thrive. I love you from the desert to the mountains, from the city to the country, across thousands of miles, and just across the room. I want the chance to prove that to you every single day. I love you more than anything in the world. Marry me? Please?" I drop to my knee in front of her and wait.

And wait.

"Yes," she whispers, tears rolling down her face.

"Yes?" I ask because she did not sound really sure about that answer.

"Yes, yes. Absolutely yes."

As delicately as I can, I slide the ring onto her finger. Her hands are kind of swollen, and the fit is tight, but that seems to be our thing.

EPILOGUE

Jack

Christmas in Mississippi

"I'LL GO." I PUSH up off the floor, pressing Mason's bare feet to my lips.

He doesn't just giggle, but he full-on belly-laughs at the raspberry I blow on them. Dix stares at me, judgment in his big brown eyes. Daring me to do the same to him, but I know better.

My boys are as identical as twins can be, but that doesn't mean they don't have different personalities. Where Mason is a foot man, Dixon is a belly boy.

I walk my fingers up the red-and-white stripes covering his chubby thighs, and little gasps start puffing out of him. Anticipation. The second my face makes contact with his belly, he howls. Laughing and snorting. Gasping, arms flailing. Fat, little fists pulling at what strands of hair they can grasp.

"Uncle Jack, do me. Gickle me," Harper pleads, flopping on the floor next to the boys.

While Kate's niece and the rest of her family have made me feel more than a part of the family, I'm still working on her old man. For a Southern gentleman with a clean-hands banking job, the man is scary as fuck when it comes to his daughter. Granted, I know I did things ass backward and need to earn his respect, but I'm at a loss here. Bourbon, cigars, hunting. I've tried everything, and there's still a chasm that screams to be bridged.

But Harper? Yep, I've got that girl on my side.

Before I can even get my fingers near her neck, she's squealing and laughing, sliding herself across the floor to escape.

"Christ, I hope that never changes," Sam mutters as his older daughter finds her feet and runs to the kitchen.

I pop to standing, the sudden movement startling Mason and Dix, their arms flinging out to the sides, eyes wide.

Sam pulls the bottle from his baby girl's mouth, slack with sleep. "You teach her to run away from boys, and Daddy'll have no choice but to come around and welcome you into the fold."

Glancing over my shoulder toward the study—because, of course, Mr. Beard has a study—I huff out a laugh. "Won't hold my breath on that. Need me to grab anything for you from the store? You wanna go with?" I offer, knowing full well the answer is a resounding—

"Hell no. You have fun with hitting that madhouse on Christmas." Shaking his head, Sam adds, "But I wouldn't say no to some beef jerky since you're going out anyway."

"Right. Didn't Jules say she didn't put any of that shit in your stocking for a reason? And what the hell makes you think you need jerky? They're in there, getting dessert ready." I slide my feet into flip-flops because Mississippi is a hell of a lot warmer than New York this time of year.

"You offered."

"That I did. Keep an eye on them, will you?" I nod at where my boys are lying on their blanket, eyes drifting closed.

Who knew I was missing a piece of my heart before they arrived? I shake the memory of that shitshow away as I lean into the kitchen. Kate, her mom, Jules, and Harper are all bustling around, getting dishes put away and desserts pulled out. Well, Harper's eating a cookie, but that's probably a strategic move to keep her occupied for a minute.

"Anything else I can grab? Diapers, for sure, but—"

Maggie pats my arm, guiding me to the door. "You just hurry on up and get those. And an extra can of whipped cream." She hands me her car keys and goes back to rearrange the platter of cookies Kate just finished making.

My wife looks exhausted, circles under the big brown eyes she shares with our boys. Lids heavy. Her smile pinched. But she couldn't be more beautiful.

I take three strides to her, unable to leave without kissing her first. "You okay?" I whisper, loving the way she sags against me, melting into my embrace.

"I'm fine"—she rubs her face and pushes her smile higher—"just tired. Hurry back, 'kay?"

I drop a kiss to her upturned lips and haul ass.

The drugstore is far busier than I thought it'd be, and grumbling, I stalk to the back of the store, praying that the refrigerator cases aren't wiped out. I grab the last can of whipped cream and scan the beer selections. Nothing worth my time, so I weave my way through the aisles to all the baby crap. I scan the shelves, zeroing in on the purple packages until I find the size to house my boys' asses. My phone buzzes with a text from Kate, asking me to get the green diapers in the same size for her littlest niece as well as a couple of bibs.

Me: Anything else?

After several seconds, there's no response, so I pick up the extra items and dump everything into a plastic basket before heading to the front of the store to check out. The line is a fucking mile long. I throw a couple of packages of jerky in the basket and settle in to wait my turn.

It's like those questions you see online. *What three things do you purchase that make the cashier wonder what's up?* Sure, my haul is tame, and I'm sitting at four items, but I chuckle at how my life has changed over the past year. Confirmed bachelor to happily married with two kids. Tense, uncomfortable Christmas at home to being welcomed with open arms by my wife's family—mostly. I'll win her dad over somehow.

My phone buzzes again, this time with a call.

"Hey, sweet cheeks. What else did you think of?" I hate to do it, but I'll step out of line, not that it's moved much.

"Jack, don't freak on me, okay?"

"What is it? What's wrong?"

"Nothing's wrong, but I just need you to stay calm and go to the back of the store. The aisle next to the baby stuff." Kate's using her teacher voice on me, and of course, it makes me want to do exactly what she asked me not to —freak out.

I stop at the head of the baby aisle and look to my right and then to my left. "Tampons or Seen on TV? Which aisle?" My heart rate slows to normal when I see the options, waiting for her reply.

"Tampon aisle, but ..."

I walk down the row, waiting for further instructions. I have no problem buying this shit, but for the life of me, I don't know what she needs. Hell, it's not like this has been a part of our relationship with pregnancy and nursing the boys.

"What do you need?"

"Um, the middle of the aisle, between the pads and the condoms," she whispers, her voice echoing like she's closed herself into a small space.

I nod to the dude standing in front of the condoms but avoid making eye contact because that's just weird. Another guy joins the first, standing closer than strictly necessary. No judgment, but damn if things don't feel a little strained all of a sudden. I turn away from them, offering some privacy, refocusing on what my wife is whispering in my ear.

"Start over, Kate. What kind do you need me to get?"

The last thing I expect is exactly what she says. "The

brand doesn't matter. Just get a damn test, Jack. I'm panicking here."

My heart swells, and I swear, my chest puffs out with pride. "Katelyn, what are you saying? Are you ... are we ..." I set the basket full of diapers on the floor and shove my hand through my hair. "How did this happen, baby? The twins are only four ..." Jesus, I can't even think. "Four months old. How? Your father's going to kill me, isn't he? I'm never getting past calling him Mr. Beard at this rate."

Kate barks out a husky laugh. "That's your big concern? That my daddy's gonna kick your ass? We're married, Jack, and at least he's not wondering if you're gay."

I pluck two different tests from the shelf, dropping them into the basket. "Yeah, no *chance* of that," I huff, putting a little emphasis on her ex's name.

A gasp shoots out of the dude with the condoms, his hand flying to his mouth. I turn to face him, wondering what the chances are that this is Chance. The *Chance*. I stare straight at him, shit-eating grin firmly in place.

"I love you more than anything in the world, Kate. Best Christmas gift, two years running. We gonna make this a thing?"

After calling me an asshole, Kate ends the call, leaving me standing between tampons and condoms, beaming like a fool.

Thank you for spending time in Beekman Hills with Jack and

Kate. I would love to know what you think of these two! If you can, please drop a quick review on your favorite retailer for me! To stay up on releases and happenings, make sure you're signed up for my newsletter at www.kcenderswrites.com

...now, jump into **Broken: A Salvation Society Novel** for the rest of Chloe Triplett's story.

PLAYLIST FOR TOMBSTONES

Hymn for the Missing - Red
Troubled Souls - Kail Baxley
Hero - Shaman's Harvest
Hail to the King - Avenged Sevenfold
Black Soul - Shinedown
Go to War - Nothing More
All of Me - Frank Sinatra
Into the Nothing - Breaking Benjamin
'Til the Casket Drops - ZZ Ward
The Time is Now – Atreyu

OTHER TITLES FROM KC ENDERS

For the most up to date information on available titles, visit my website at www.kcenderswrites.com and be sure to sign up for my newsletter.

Beekman Hills Series
Troubles
Twist
Tombstones

Stand Alone Titles
Sweet on You
Broken: A Salvation Society Novel

The UnBroken Series
In Tune *(formerly Tunes)*
Off Bass
Coming Soon:

ACKNOWLEDGMENTS

ACKNOWLEDGMENTS HAVE NEVER BEEN all that difficult to write. This one, though is tough. Really tough and I have avoided it for longer than was practical or wise. This book, Tombstones, was planned a long time ago. Really since the idea that maybe, just maybe I could write a book—make that three—and if all went well, a handful of people might read it/them. Well, you all have gone above and beyond my wildest imagination in your kind words, recommendations and general excitement for my words. Honestly...what have I done to deserve this? The timing with this one is where things get tricky and emotional.

I started writing Tombstones, back in late September... early October and by the end of October learned that a family member was diagnosed with an aggressive cancer. He fought hard, but cancer sucks and just this morning he passed away. He was a bit of a Francie McBride, Irish as the day is long and always giving and caring for others. He left this world a better place for having been in it

I'd like to thank the amazing family I have. Typically, I dedicate my books to *My Fiends* — my husband and boys who support me like crazy in this writing thing. But family is so much more, and I have been blessed with the best of the best. Thank you.

Okay, then. Thank you to Jovanna at Unforeseen Editing for polishing and prettying and making my words better. Thank you to Judy at Proofreading by Judy for making things perfect. And Alora Kate for blowing me away with this cover—holy hotness! I count you all among my blessings.

Deedy, thank you for more than I can even say; keeping my Pinterest boards fresh, brainstorming the funniest damn scenes, including one that ended up being absolutely pivotal to the story! You keep me motivated and sane and on track and all of that! Thank you from the bottom of my heart.

McKinzee, Robin, Alamea, Jenn, and Mel—much love for reading this and helping me to make it better.

M & C, thank you. Your friendship and means the world to me. I'm not sure what I did to deserve you, but I thank God that I have you.

Aerin for naming Jess. Stacy for the memes, check ins and word count reminders.

The bloggers who took time to post and promote this book. My ARC team for all your excitement and spreading the word. Your reviews and recommendations touch my heart and fill my soul. Thank you.

And then there are all the 'patrons' at McBride's on Main—my reader group. I can't tell you how much I enjoy each and every one of you! I'm thankful you've found me and can't imagine the place without you!! Thank you.

ABOUT THE AUTHOR

Karin is a New York Girl living in a Midwest world. A connoisseur of great words, fine bourbon, and strong coffee, she's married to the love of her life and is mother to two grown men that she is proud to say can cook and clean up after themselves, and always open doors for the ladies thanks to the Rules of Being a Gentleman (you're welcome, world).

Her one major vice is rescuing and adopting big dogs. Tons of personality, not so good on manners.

She loves talking books, hearing from readers, and hosting the occasional virtual Happy Hour in her reading group.

www.kcenderswrites.com

facebook.com/kcewrites

instagram.com/authorkcenders

Made in the USA
Monee, IL
09 July 2023